Reader Be Thou Also Ready

Cover photographs: house by Phyllis Blades © 1986; William Fawcett gravestone by Joe Blades © 1999.
Page 9: William Fawcett gravestone phoptotgraph by Deborah Trask, History Collection, Nova Scotia Museum, Halifax. Used by permission.
Design and in-house editing by Joe Blades.

Printed and bound in Canada by VISTAinfo, Scarborough

Broken Jaw Press
Box 596 Stn A
Fredericton NB E3B 5A6
Canada

www.brokenjaw.com
tel / fax 506 454-5127
jblades@nbnet.nb.ca

Canadian Cataloguing in Publication Data
James, Robert, 1946-

Reader be thou also ready

ISBN 1-896647-26-X

1. Fawcett, William, d. 1832 — Fiction. I. Title.

PS8569.A462R43 2000   C813'.54   C00-950034-0
PR9199.3.J37698R3 2000

Robert James

Reader Be Thou Also Ready

Fredericton • Canada

Dedication

This book is dedicated to my wife, Sandra. It is only with her love, support and encouragement that it could be written.

Acknowledgements

Thanks to Kathy Lewis who, through her assembling of the genealogy and history of the Fawcett family, provided much of the factual framework for this story. It was her recording of the facts that stimulated me to provide the answers to the many unanswered questions.

Fawcett historians will note that I changed the names of some of the family members. This was done to avoid confusion and make the story more readable. As a work of historical fiction, the events are factual but their interpretation and embellishment is fiction.

I owe a special debt of gratitude to my wife's sister, Sheila, and her husband, Ross, who read the early chapters and, by their enthusiasm, encouraged me to continue writing and to email them each new chapter.

My mother and Sandra's mother were very supportive and I appreciate the gentleness of their perceptive criticisms.

I would never hear the end of it if I didn't thank Tracy and Brian for just being Tracy and Brian. I love you guys.

Here lies the Body of WILLIAM FAWCETT who was a plain industrious hospitable & deeply pious man whose uniformly Christian conduct gained him the respect of all who became acquainted with him. While reading one of M[r] Wesley's Sermons, his immortal spirit was instantly precipitated into the Eternal world to take posession of his final rest by some monster of iniquity that will be discovered at the last day who intentionally shot him dead through the kitchen window on the evening of June 19th, 1832 in the 63[d] Year of his Age.

Reader be thou also ready.

— Old Methodist Burying Ground, Middle Sackville, New Brunswick

Photo by Deborah Trask, History Collection, Nova Scotia Museum, Halifax.

Chapter I

James felt her hand slip into his as they stood in silence. He gave a little squeeze. How had it come to this? How had he let it come to this? All his life he had taken charge, gained control, and now he was helpless. He had let them down. A life rested in someone else's hands and he could do no more.

His wife looked up into his eyes and attempted a smile. Her weak attempt was somehow pathetic in its failure, yet, her face reflected such strength. He depended on that strength, relied on it, lived for it. At the same time, the sparkle and the tenderness still shone through. He always felt that it was her eyes. God he loved her. Why was it so hard to tell her that?

Looking at the woman on his other side, he marveled at the similarities — the raven black hair, the way the corners of their mouths threatened to turn up into a grin at the tiniest opportunity and the eyes. People said that she was her mother's daughter, and it was because of the eyes.

In only three short days, he become familiar with this room as they sat behind the wooden railing like cattle watching life on the other side of the fence. How many other sweaty hands had gripped this same bar, waiting for twelve men to decide a destiny?

It was the waiting, the same thoughts and the same questions permeating every second, every minute and every hour. The last two hours had been the worst — not knowing, just waiting.

The judge motioned to the foreman, who stood, a grave look on his face. Three days ago there had been no Josiah Hicks, this little man with the wispy gray hair who was now the centre of attention. Josiah was enjoying his moment, savouring the respect of everyone who stared at him in this crowded courtroom.

"May we have the verdict?"

James thought back to a similar little man who had commanded and demanded a similar deference. He thought back to a particular day when he was only thirteen years old, so long ago. So much had happened.

He slumped in the school desk, pushed down with his toes in his worn black, leather shoes and forced his knees up painfully against the bottom of the wooden writing surface. The bench groaned as it tipped against the weight of the other students but he was conscious only of the pain in his legs. Through performing this ritual, he hoped to add some stimulation to the otherwise passive activity of the geography lesson in the one-room schoolhouse.

Glancing up at the black-robed schoolmaster, he let his eyes drift to the stuffed crow perched on top of the battered wooden cabinet. By quickly shutting one eye and then the other, he could make the crow move and hop down on the head of Mr. Gallagher where it dug its talons into his stringy hair. Blood spurted through the tangled, gray thatch while he hopped around and around the raised platform at the front of the room, screaming and flapping his arms in time with the beating of the wings of the avenging black bird. Was the crow now part of Gallagher or was he wearing some bizarre Indian headdress?

"Mr. George. Mr. George! Would you care to illuminate us with your insight on this problem?"

James quickly wiped the drool from the corner of his mouth and jumped out of his seat opposite to where the teacher was standing. Suddenly alert, he became conscious of the little specks of spit flying from the master's mouth, of the dry patch in his own throat, of the snickers and taunts of the boys and muffled giggles of the girls, and of the embarrassed red heat spreading rapidly from his ears down his cheeks to his neck.

"Caw. Er, no, sir. I mean, yes, sir. I don't know, sir. That is..., could you repeat the question, sir?"

Aware of the familiar burning in his eyes, the knot deep in his throat, and the bubble forming between his parted lips, he knew that he was starting to cry. He hated when it happened and he hated himself for letting it happen. Worst was that it provided ammunition for additional teasing from the other boys, especially from the boys at the home.

"Perhaps if you were to remain standing for the rest of the afternoon you would be better able to keep your attention on the lessons at hand and be less apt to dream. Maybe six of the best would sharpen your senses." The long, thin pointer bounced lively in his hand to better emphasize and punctuate every word.

James stared through blurred eyes, sniffled back the tears, and watched the old clock which hung above the blackboard. He tried to anticipate the exact moment that there would be a loud click and the larger hand would bounce forward to the next minute. If he concentrated on this he might possibly avoid blubbering like a baby.

He said the plea over in his mind, the one he always said, "Oh please God, help me God. Help me God. I promise I won't do it again. I promise." This was not so much a prayer as another ritual to be said for luck. Once again there was no answer, no relief. He thought bitterly, "Not even God cares."

Trudging back to the home beside Peter, he was ready for his older brother to start in on him again.

"You really have to pay attention in class and you have got to control that crying. You are such a baby. You're thirteen years old now and you should know better. Everybody's talking about you, making fun of you. It makes me look stupid, too"

They walked along in silence. James kept his head down looking at his worn shoes causing puffs of dust in the path through the woods.

He liked it better when it was summer and they went barefoot all the time. Now they had to wear shoes. Changing his gait only to kick the occasional tiny pine cone, he thought about Peter, two years older, who had been acting differently the last few weeks. He still didn't talk to him at school, somehow pretending that they weren't related and giving the impression that if he didn't talk to him maybe nobody would know. He didn't really mind Peter ignoring him as they had never been that close anyway.

They had always fought, but since their deaths, the only family that he had left was Peter who seemed to find some measure of solace in taking responsibility for the younger boy as if by doing what they would have wished, he might be able to maintain a connection with them. To Peter, this was his job, his duty.

James felt his cap slip forward over his eyes as he stumbled into him. A handful of dry grass floated down over his worn, gray coat accompanied by the cry, "Alms for the poor! Alms for the poor." The other boys rushed past laughing and taunting.

"Damn your eyes, Billy Colpitts." The epithet was one that his father had told him was common on the British Man-of-Wars and James was proud to use it. He sailed a stone at the fleeing backs of the young lads who were already safely out of range. "You're dead tomorrow." He wasn't angry. Suddenly, he felt better that he was doing something, taking control again. In throwing the stone he had acted, not like at school where he had been weak and passive. Now he was back in charge.

James pulled his cap forward, a little lower on his eyes than he usually wore it. He looked up from under the brim into his brother's eyes and the words tumbled out. "I'm leaving, Peter. I can't stand it any more. I hate the home. It didn't used to be like this. We had friends. We were a family. People weren't mean to us. Why did he have to die, anyway? It was her fault. It was her stupid idea to leave. It was all her fault. If mother were alive...."

Peter stopped. He put his hands on the shoulders of his brother's jacket and yelled, "Well, she's not alive. She's dead. Father's dead. They're all dead." His fingers tightened on the gray wool as if he were trying to press the truths home. To James it only added to the weight of the world that he was already carrying.

Peter softened his voice. "You have to accept it. You have to learn to get along. You can't fight every Billy Colpitts. You can't fight the world. Things will work out, just you wait and see. Things could be worse. It won't be forever. We have a place to sleep, and food to eat in the home."

"Poorhouse," James whispered. A cold breeze rustled through the trees, swirled the leaves on the path and made the New Brunswick fall day seem a little more desolate. "It isn't a home. A home is what we had before. It's a poorhouse. "

The remainder of the walk was taken in silence. This silence could be misinterpreted as an agreement or a truce but they both knew that nothing had been solved. They hadn't changed their minds and they hadn't altered their opinions.

Peter let his mind go blank because it was easier that way. It didn't hurt as much.

James, however, thought of the small pack hidden under the straw bales in the stable at the back of the home. In it he had begun to place the things he would need for his trip, his escape.

Chapter II

Actually, the home was a new and modern facility, the pride of the community as it was a frame building, one of the new styles, with the lumber coming from a local mill with two chimneys signifying two fireplaces which was a luxury beyond measure in the early 1800's. Some said that its erection had caused no little bit of displeasure from John Humphrey, the blacksmith who had just built a two fireplace, four room log home that was the envy of all. However, this home was a tangible sign of the progressive, growing community of Sackville and it signified different things, most of them positive.

The cost and labour had been a cooperative effort of the various churches which, with their distinct dogmas and congregations, were located in separate structures throughout the town. As well, the government had contributed its blessing and financial support to this endeavour. Orphans had been the responsibility of the family in England, so an aunt or uncle, grandparent or other relative would care for them or there were always the workhouses and poorhouses, but these buildings generally housed those who were destitute. In this new land, children without parents were a real problem since the nearest relative was often thousands of miles and an ocean away. Existing families were having sufficient difficulty surviving the establishment of a new life in this harsh land without adding another mouth to feed, especially without the promise of eventual reward. They needed boys who would stay and work the land. The building of this home put a solution to the problem and the people of Sackville could demonstrate a Christian charity that benefited their own community.

The inside of the building was divided into four rooms but for James and the other boys it might as well have been two for that was all they ever saw. The living area was more of an eating area, a large table surrounded by chairs being the dominant feature. The fireplace, cupboards and shelves were really part of the walls and were not conspicuous at first inspection since apart from the single glass window, only the dishes and cooking utensils provided a break from the mass of wood. The floor was made of new yellow planks, quickly taking on a distinctive patina as dirt and daily living were ground into the central areas. The rafters spread out from a huge, central beam that displayed the individual adze cuts of the men who fashioned it. Someone had calculated and allowed for the tremendous snow loads of the area and had built it accordingly.

When the boys arrived from school, they had chores to do so they changed into their work clothes and went about their assigned tasks. James worked in the barn today which suited him fine, anything but kitchen duty. He forked the manure into the barrow being careful not to include too much straw as this would bring comments of wastefulness from Edgar, the outside man. He cleaned and refilled the water buckets, broke open more hay for the mangers and poured a measure of oats into the horses' feeding troughs.

After raking the common areas and entryways he hustled back to check his pack hidden under the straw. He fondled the white bone jackknife, a present from his father last Christmas and carefully caressed the British army crest on its case. Opening the blade, he ran the edge across his thumbnail watching the tiny, white shavings pile up in front of the keen blade. He remembered, as he always did, his father warning him that a dull knife was more dangerous than a sharp one. At the same time Mrs. Anderson had been saying that he was too young to have a knife. To James, this was more than a knife, it was a memory of his father.

He nestled the treasure back in the bottom of the pack at the same time checking the bits of twine, the flint, the broken piece of mirrored glass, the two apples and the biscuits which were part of his preparations. The dinner bell interrupted his dreaming and, wistfully stuffing the pack under the straw, he headed for supper, grabbing an armful of kindling from the woodshed on his way.

The boys could tell what day it was by the menu and today was pie day. One's current relationship with Mrs. Fisher, the cook and house mother, determined the size of your portion and James received a medium slice. He had long since stopped trying to identify the kind of meat inside the crust but rather stuffed it in his mouth, washed it down with large slurps of milk and enjoyed every mouthful.

After supper was finished and the dishes cleaned there was time to do homework and gather wood for the night. The younger boys trooped off for bath night so he was spared that humiliation and instead he watched Mrs. Fisher sewing squares of material for a quilt while some of the boys played, talked or read quietly. Whatever he decided to do there was one constant, there was no privacy from the other lads. With nowhere to go to be by yourself or to be alone, there were few secrets in the home.

This first room opened into the sleeping area but, to better allow the heat from the fireplaces to find its way to the other parts of the home, no door separated the two areas. Likewise, no ceilings capped the walls that divided the building into sections. Twenty identical beds, ten to each side, lined the long walls. The head of each bed was at the wall and the foot stuck out into the room allowing a narrow aisle down the middle. Making the best use of space, the beds were shoved together in twos with a single wood chair marking the exact width of the separation between each pair while stretching halfway of the length between each pair of beds was a thin wooden partition which rose up two feet above the beds, but it gave a little privacy for the sleeping boys. The short wall opposite the doorway held a bank of drawers which housed their clothes and possessions. Although two small windows perched above these, they were only reachable if you climbed up on the top of the built-in dressers so they remained open or closed for seasons at a time.

Such were the furnishings of the home. Very adequate and very utilitarian, as were the furnishings of most of the houses at this time. However, there was a major difference that distinguished this home from the other residences in Sackville and this difference did not escape James. This residence belied its name. Everyone knew it as "the home" but it was a house, not a home. Absent were all those niceties that make a habitation unique. There was no piece of artwork, no cross-stitch sampler, no painting, no carved work, or no heirloom. There was no doily on the table, no afghan thrown carelessly over the chair, no hand sewn pillow on the settee, no trophy of the hunt, no family Bible on the stand, no china vase, no hand-painted water pitcher or basin. There was no rag mat at the door, no homey verse on the wall, or no frilly sheer curtain. There was no rifle at the ready by the fireplace, no worn leather coat hanging on a peg, no clay pipe in a dish by a favourite chair, no pretty bottle of smelly rose water and no mother and no father.

Promptly at nine they stoked the fires and snuffed the candles. Some welcomed the long, dark night while others feared it and James did both. He welcomed the quiet and the peace of the night but he dreaded that time when he awoke every night, alone and in panic, and would cry as he lay and prayed that he might fall back to sleep. The shadows loomed with new horrors, sounds intensified and nobody heard him cry out, no one comforted him or sang to him or kissed his forehead.

Lying quietly, he heard John Stevens, the boy in the next bed, whisper under the partition. "Where you from?"

"Me? My father was an officer in the British army and we got some land up the Saint John River Valley where we had a farm and did some lumbering. How about you?"

"My parents got the fever and died on the ship from Liverpool to Halifax. My aunt and uncle are coming to look after me. They'll be here soon. What happened to your parents?"

James sighed. "My mother died of fever two years ago and my father married this lady named Mrs. Anderson. We lived on the farm except she didn't like it so they decided we would all move west. Some of her relatives are there. She wasn't really my mother but we all had to go."

"You were lucky," John replied. "At least you got to live on a farm. So what happened?"

Reluctantly at first, James began to tell the story of how they had piled all their belongings into the little boat and had left their home. His father had sold the animals and the farm implements as well as his prized crosscut saw but their remaining possessions still overloaded the small boat and the river was rough. What started as an adventure developed into a tragedy.

The fun of the trip turned to boredom as the day wore on and the boys were restless. James and Peter had been arguing and fighting in the bow of the boat and, despite threats of punishment, they began to poke each other. In order to separate them, Mrs. Anderson stood to trade places with one of the boys and however it had happened, perhaps she had caught her long, layered dress or maybe she had tripped on one of the many bundles on the floor boards, she lost her balance and, as she fell against the low gunwale, she tumbled out of the boat into the frigid river.

Piercing the stillness of the day, her screams, mixed with unintelligible gurgles, were clearly distinguishable above the roar and smash of the watery torrent. Without hesitation, their father dove into the raging waves which seemed to reach out and welcome him with icy fingers as he dared to try and alter destiny. As he battled the current attempting to reach and rescue her, he commanded the panicked boys, "Stay in the boat. Don't move."

Now that he had started to tell the story, James barely paused to catch his breath. He related to John how it seemed for awhile that all might end as simply another five minute story of danger and rescue to tell his friends. However the line between danger and disaster is subtle and you never really know whether you have approached it or have crossed it. Whether it was fate or bad luck, they crossed the line that day.

As the water swirled them around and the brothers tried in vain to maneuver the boat back to the drama, her cries of help got weaker and weaker. Her dress ballooned around her and over her and the last picture that he had in his mind was that of the wet material smothering his father, the soggy cloth showing the outline of his distraught face, the man unable to catch a breath. The wet clothes and the heavy shoes worked to drag them down like an anchor and, as they sank below the surface of the water which silenced their shouts, only a few bubbles were left to prove that anything had been amiss. It all had taken place in less time than it took to tell the story.

James told John how his brother and he had sat there, alone in the boat, neither boy saying anything. Words were not necessary as they both knew.

"What did you do then? Couldn't you save them?"

"We knew they had drowned. Nobody has to tell you, you just know. We rowed the boat to shore and followed the shore line. We hadn't passed any houses so we kept going. We left the boat and pushed through the bush."

James shared his tale of a nightmarish escape from the angry waters, the running, the stumbling, the crying and the sobbing. They didn't know where they were going or what they were going to do when they got there. Covered with mud and scrapes they came to a farm where, in a flood of tears and grief, they gushed out the hapless adventure to the young couple who lived there. The rest was a blur that he couldn't remember.

Of course, it was too late to do anything to save the parents so the couple tried to comfort the two orphans. James didn't know what was going to happen to them and didn't care. For awhile he thought that they might allow them to stay there but the people subsequently arranged for someone to transport the boys from Saint John to the home in Sackville. He wasn't clear on how it had all happened as it was a muddle in his mind. He wasn't conscious of either the passage of time or events but simply obeyed the directions of the various adults, going wherever and doing whatever they told him without either comment or protest.

It was only recently that he began to take stock of his situation and began to reclaim control of his life. Unfortunately he manifested this by many acts of disobedience as well as a growing disregard for authority as he slipped into his own little world where he felt nothing and trusted no one.

Now that he had finally told the account of his parents' death, James felt somehow relieved. Maybe this was the catharsis that he needed.

"Wow, that's quite a story. You must have been scared. I know I would have been," John empathized.

"Don't tell anybody. I kind of don't like anybody else to know."

"Don't worry. I won't say a word to anyone. It'll be our secret. What's going to happen to you?"

"I don't know. Nobody tells me anything."

Here was a friend with whom he could share secrets and talk. The weight of the guilt might not be quite so unbearable and maybe everything was going to turn out fine. James slept through the night for the first time since the drowning.

Chapter III

The next few weeks were some of the happiest in James's recent memory as he and John Stevens were inseparable. They ate their breakfast together, they walked and talked to school together, they even volunteered for activities in the classroom that would allow them to be with one another. Often they traded parts of their lunches or, at least, ate them while sitting side by side by the swings. They managed to persuade Mrs. Fisher to give them chores that allowed them to banter back and forth or tease each other or simply keep one another in sight. James was happy again and even imagined that Mrs. Fisher was giving him slightly larger portions of pudding or pie.

Some of their escapades were typical boys' pranks. John had heard that red was supposed to anger bulls so they decided to test the theory. They borrowed a pair of red flannel underwear from the clothesline outside the home and stowed them safely in John's school bag for later use. They were both on their best behaviour at school that day so that Mr. Gallagher wouldn't keep them in after dismissal. Clambering up and over the stone fence by the Maxwell farm and bending low so that no one would see them, they ran along the barrier until they were next to the victims of their experiment.

"When I say, you jump up and wave the flag. Ready? Now!"

They sprang up together and waved their challenge. The herd took a couple of stutter steps.

"Let's get the hell out of here. Whoa! They're coming after us."

It would be difficult to say if the boys or the milk cows were more startled. Dropping their red cloth, the boys chased each other home wrestling and laughing, arguing about who was the bigger chicken. For weeks after, a genuine puzzle existed that created quite a few grins around the county for no one was quite sure how Edgar's underwear ended up on Maxwell's fence.

Another day, James and John hustled away from the schoolhouse and took refuge on the hill by Morice's Pond where they pulled up several tufts of long fall grass complete with roots and earth and arranged them in a row. Waiting patiently until Rebecca and Betsy Tingley passed on the path below they pretended that they were a British bomb ship as they lobbed the clods of earth down on the unsuspecting girls.

"Bombs away. We're the British! Bomb the frogs!" With blood-curdling cries they peppered the girls who were relegated to playing the role of French forts. Pointing at the girls who were shaking their fists and vowing revenge, John screamed, "Look at them run. We rule the seas."

Later that evening, after Mrs. Tingley visited the home, the boys didn't even seem to care when Mr. Fisher administered the appropriate punishment with his famous switch.

"It was worth it," James said. "It didn't hurt anyway."

The boys shared everything from the smallest little detail to their most grandiose plans. John told him of his first days in Halifax where there was no home, but rather poor rates or taxes were collected to cover the cost of the care for the poor and infirm, including orphans, and the community would pay from its funds for someone to take an underage orphan into their home as a servant. Placement would go to the lowest bidder so the family that would accept the least money to provide room and board for this homeless child would get him. This waif could be used as labour on the farm or in the business as if he were a family member — unpaid, of course.

John explained that because he was fourteen he was not in great demand for this type of adoption as soon he would be considered to be of age and would be able to strike out on his own, so no one would want to take a chance. As a result, he felt fortunate to be at the home in Sackville.

"I might have been able to get a job as a ship's boy but I would have been better off if I were a girl," he complained. "Girls get jobs as servants or, if they are pretty enough, they can marry a soldier." He explained to a wide-eyed James how they would become informal wives for the soldiers at the British garrisons in Halifax. They could be legally married in a church and the children would be considered legitimate. However, the marriage was not recognized by the Royal Army and therefore the wife was not shipped on to the soldier's next posting. So the marriage lasted the term of the soldier's stay in Halifax, followed by abandonment.

"What a great deal!" James exclaimed. "They get to have a wife with no strings attached. Why do the girls do it?"

Proud that he had some great information to share, John enlightened him, "They aren't stupid. There's all kinds of them that'll do it just so they don't have to stay on the farm their whole life. That's even worse!"

James visited his hidden knapsack only once during this time and that was to show John his treasures. He even let him hold and open the knife. John's eyes said everything as he caressed the raised crest with envy and ran his fingers lovingly down its length. In a hushed tone he whispered reverently, "If you ever get tired of this, I'll take it off your hands."

"I have to keep it sharp," James told him, "A dull knife is more dangerous than a sharp one." He, too, was eager to show that he knew something.

Each boy took the knife in turn and pricked the end of his thumb. Holding them together so that the blood mingled, John confided, "Now we are Indian blood brothers. No matter what happens we will always be friends until the day we die. This is really what they do, you know."

"I know," whispered James. He didn't know, but if John said so, it was good enough for him. They took off their shirts and ran around letting out war whoops. For a couple of days they called each other "Lone Feather" and "Crying Wolf" and secretly showed each other the pigeon feathers that they carried in their pockets as badges of their tribe.

Although James shared with John his plans for running away and even suggested that they might do so together, these thoughts of escape weren't infiltrating his every waking hour as they had been. "Don't tell anybody about it," he warned. "I may stick around for a bit longer, anyway."

For now, life at the home was fine, except for the teasing. The pecking order was well established and one's position improved as you got older. Ordinary boys can be cruel to each other but some of these home boys were barbarous. The experiences and rejections which had already been part of their young lives, made them quite hardened and heartless. James hadn't been alone long enough to establish the veneer which would make it seem to others that the words and actions didn't bother him. Sadly, it was that which had lately made him the most happy that now began to cause him the most grief, his friendship with John.

It began with comments like "There go the twins" and progressed to "Which one's the bride and which one's the groom?" Now it was getting nasty with the older boys taunting,

"Do you shake it for him after he takes a leak?" Or after the candles were out, "What's that creaking? I thought their beds were separated." Some even began to making kissing noises every time the boys were seen together. If James found these innuendoes disturbing, John found them intolerable and, in this environment, there was no relief and no escape.

Things came undone one bath night. The six half barrels were pulled into the corner of the bedroom and filled with warm water by means of many trips to and from the fireplace. As the boys whose turn it was for a bath got quickly undressed, each found a tub. James was careful to turn to the wall and hold his wash cloth strategically in front as he slipped into the water.

"Hey, why don't you guys jump in the same tub?"

"Here's some soap to make it more fun."

"Hey, John. How come you hang around with that little sissy anyway?"

John looked around at all the older boys teasing him and then stared at James huddled alone in the bath. He made a decision in a split second to sacrifice his friend for the sake of acceptance by the others. He was young and there really was no choice. "I was just feeling sorry for him, guys. I don't really like him. It's just that his parents drowned."

John didn't plan for what was going to transpire next, it just happened. He sensed the others grab this new piece of information as vultures pounce on a scrap of meat and begin to twist it around to use it in their next salvo of jibes.

"Drowned? Was the water too high in the bath, Jamie?"

"What happened? Did the officer march through a puddle?"

"Is that why you don't wash your face, James?"

With each new taunt, the laughter got louder. The boys were relentless as they continued to encourage each other with more and more spiteful comments at James's expense. John realized what he had done to his friend and perhaps he should have been sorry but he was a survivor and recognized a golden opportunity to repurchase the older boys' favour at James's expense. He saw how easy it had been to regain their respect with one little tidbit of information, the thought of how he might grow in esteem with the rest of the secrets, was just too tempting. He had a lot more information that he could provide.

"He says that his dad drowned in his stepmother's dress."

The other boys howled in laughter

With that John took his wash cloth, placed it over his face and began gurgling and burbling as he sank down into the tub demonstrating a parody of what had happened in the Saint John River. He raised up out of the water and, allowing the water to bubble out of his mouth, he gargled, "Help me. I'm drowning." With arms flailing he sank under the surface again, rose up and, with his mouth, he aimed a spurt of water across at James who was absolutely motionless, refusing to believe what he was witnessing. The hoots of the other boys spurred John on to more mimicking of his friend and, like a performer responding to a curtain call, he could not help himself, he couldn't stop. The hilarity persisted with the young boy as the brunt of the laughter.

Mercifully, it didn't matter any more. The roar in his head, the pulsing in his temples, blocked out the meaning of the words. He was beyond anymore hurt as all the feelings of insecurity and abandonment flooded back. The deception of all those he had loved invaded his brain — first, his mother, then his father, and now his friend. He had trusted each of them and each had deserted him, let him down.

When the pounding in his head stopped, he felt empty but this time he didn't cry. Maybe all along, he had been expecting John to do something like this and it wasn't really a surprise when it happened. He was more angry with himself than with John for he was a fool to think that everything was going to be fine, he should have known better. Trust no one, only yourself, feel nothing, use people before they used you, these were the lessons that he had learned, would remember and follow because he knew what he must do and he would do it tonight.

Many of the habits that children follow are set activities that parents reinforce at various times of the day such as washing before meals or a story or prayers at bedtime. These are comforting and bring order to a child's life. The loss of these comforts at the death of his mother, intensified by the termination of the remaining ones when his father and Mrs. Anderson drowned, had left a large void in James's life. As youth are blessed by a resilience which manufactures solutions to help overcome life's deficiencies, he began inventing, or perhaps discovering, his own set of rituals to provide rudders for the hard times, the little prayers and promises to God, the way that he always moved himself into the same position in his bed to help himself fall to sleep at night, and the habit of flipping his pillow every time it got warm so that he would have a cool surface under his head.

That night he did not worry that he would not wake up in the middle of the night. Thanks to his friend John, he knew that the course of sleeping through the nights had ended with a certainty.

When he opened his eyes, he did not know what time it was but he knew that the time was right. His bare feet never hit the cold floor as he had gone to sleep wearing all his clothes. He stuffed his pillow under the covers to resemble a sleeping body, the way children have for years. Grabbing his shoes, cap, jacket and a few extra things, he slowly and quietly walked the length of the room serenaded by the various sounds of sleeping. Originally, James had planned to sneak out one of the windows, but he realized there was no need for such stealth as a boy going outside to relieve himself in the night was a common enough occurrence.

Safely outside, he finished dressing, looked around and relocated the familiar landmarks. Complete darkness does not exist in the woods at night, so he waited until his eyes were accustomed to the low light and then made his way to the barn. As the door screeched stubbornly, resisting on its hinges, he paused and stood absolutely still. He could see his breath in front of his face but all was quiet. He waited expecting a challenge but all he heard was the far off bark of a dog answered shortly by another wail from a different quarter. Putting his cache of clothes on the ground he slipped inside the barn where again he stopped and waited. He heard noises that he could identify as the horses or cows moving restlessly and other unidentifiable sounds from animals that he could only imagine, scurrying about in the hay.

As he stole quickly to the corner of the straw mound and thrust his hand under the bales to retrieve his pack, his mind was working quickly and he was eager to be on his way. His fingers probed and prodded through the chaff. He quickened his search. Was this the right place? He dug deeper, his heart pounding and the wetness spreading from his armpits. With both hands he continued like a terrier puppy on the chase of some burrowing rodent, the straw and dust rising in a frantic fury above as he pushed his hands deeper and deeper into the straw. Up to his elbows, he refused to accept the obvious, maybe he had been confused. He looked around to check his bearings and began groping again. James widened the area of his search long after he knew it was hopeless until finally, with a sob, he fell back into a sitting position where he tucked his head between his knees, wrapped his arms around his legs and rocked back and forth in absolute dejection. Things had reached the absolute bottom, life was hardly worth living.

He sat for what seemed like a long time, his body convulsing in silent spasms. Then he stood and said aloud, "You bastard."

He moved back to the door of the home where he again removed his shoes and sneaked back into the sleeping quarters. He briefly considered dropping on him and simply pummeling him for all he was worth but he knew a more fitting punishment. Going over to the chair beside his bed he picked up John's clothes, checking the pockets unsuccessfully for any sign of the knife. He felt around under the bed until he located both shoes and carefully tucked everything into John's school bag which was already filled with books. Satisfied, he headed back outside.

James didn't stop to put on his own shoes but walked straight to the back of the home and directly into the outhouse. Without any hesitation, he stuffed all of John's belongings down one of the openings and then, for good measure, unbuttoned his fly and pissed down the hole after them.

After putting on his shoes and gathering what was left of his own clothing, he turned his back on the home and he headed into the woods.

Chapter IV

It would be charitable to say that James knew what he was going to do now, he had no idea. He had no plan and he had nowhere to go. He was a young boy who had run away from home, the home, the only home that he now had and, like thousands of boys who had run away before him and thousands of boys would run away after him, part of James wanted someone to stop him and to beg him not to go. He wished that they would tell him they were sorry and they knew they had been mean to him. They would plead with him to return because now they were going to be nice to him and reluctantly, he would go back and life would be better.

Another part of him wanted to teach them a lesson. They would awake, see him gone and feel guilty for the way they had treated him and they'd be sorry. He might not even forgive them just to show them. He wanted to believe that they really did care.

However, for boys like James, it is doubtful if anyone really did care. No one would list him as a fugitive because he wasn't escaping from an indentured situation. No one had paid for his services and, frankly, there were a lot of boys in similar circumstances. He was a liability and if he were so unappreciative to run away then just let him try to succeed out there on his own at thirteen years of age. Another, more deserving, would quickly take his spot in the home. But James didn't know that and it was probably better that he continued under the delusion that someone was really interested in what happened to him.

As he headed into the woods, his first thought was to put sufficient distance between the home and himself to make pursuit difficult, so he moved as quickly as possible, stumbling and floundering from tree to tree. The darkness made progress difficult as he could not pick out all the small branches which seemed to whip across his face so he adopted the practice of moving with one arm out in front of his forehead to ward off the stinging twigs. Regardless, more than once they caused welts as a result of his unsuccessful defenses and he would cry out in pain.

More of a problem was his inability to discern the undulations and depressions in the terrain which tend to level out in poor light so sometimes his toe would stub an unseen rock or catch in a unobserved root causing him to trip or fall. Worse was when he would come upon an unnoticed hole or cavity and he would collapse forward like a drunk missing the bottom step of a flight of stairs. As well as the resulting jolt, it left him with a sick feeling in his gut or he would drop on all fours, scraping his hands or tearing his knees.

More than once he called out, "I don't care. I hate you and I'm not going back." But if the animals heard him, they were too busy with their own problems of survival to be concerned about a lost runaway.

James could have handled the falling and the chill of the air except for the fact that he had never before faced the disorientation of the night. Paths that he had played on yesterday were now unfamiliar and trees that he had climbed and hid among were now unrecognizable. He was actually fleeing north, in an area north of Morice's Mill Pond that was mostly woods and marsh and it had never occurred to him that he would have been safer and just as concealed had he taken one of the main roads that night. Before dawn he would have put miles between himself and his former life but, instead, he twisted and turned to avoid impassable thickets or to circle bogs and marshes and he retraced his steps often passing the same area without a hint of recognition. Had he wished to call a halt to this escapade and to return to the relative comfort of his bed, he couldn't, for now he was lost; he had no idea where he was or where to go.

From almost the beginning of his flight, his shoes were soaked and his wool socks were cold and clammy against the shriveling skin of his feet. His legs were bruised and scraped and hurt from the twists and bangs of the missed steps and uneven footing. His face, arms and hands were lacerated and completely chilled yet the sweat trickled down his body, particularly his back. Despite these hurts and discomforts, he was not crying from his pain nor was he panicked by his unfamiliar surroundings. James would not have gone back even if he had the option.

Tears and the horror came to him when he was trapped by the inability to act, not when he made a decision — as questionable as it might be — and was acting upon it. Thinking was not a comfortable pastime for James. To this point in his life he was used to reacting to situations as they arose, not in planning or determining the course of his life. Adults had always done that for him. In battle, he would have preferred to have been the one to lead the charge and determine the consequences later, not that he made his best decisions this way, but up to now he just didn't have a lot of experience with any other way of surviving. So, James just kept walking.

Occasionally he stopped and whispered, "God help me out of this and I promise to be better." He'd then think to himself, "If there is a God then I'll be out of these woods after the next hill." The forest continued.

Although, the sun had not yet risen, he had the conscious realization that it was becoming lighter. The trees, the bushes and even the ground took on more definition. He could see colours instead of just shades of gray. It was easier to pick his way through the underbrush and around wet spots without the constant tripping and stumbling.

As well, his stomach was gurgling, reminding him that it had been awhile since he had last eaten. "If only I had thought to grab some food from the kitchen before I left," he scolded himself. Although life had been difficult for young James, he had not missed many meals and he was usually quite comfortable.

There were other happenings which took his mind off the missed breakfast. The scurryings of chipmunks and other small animals stirred the fallen leaves, noisy squirrels noted his presence and passed the news down the line, but his favourite was the small chick-a-dees that flitted frantically from bough to bough feasting on the plentiful fall berries and seeds. He loved to hear their cheerful cry. These things served to buoy his spirits and keep him going.

As he began to feel better about his situation he slowed for he thought that he heard something. He walked deliberately, choosing carefully where to place his feet. He could discern a new noise, a different noise, above all the other forest sounds. It was a clanging like that of a dinner triangle calling the workers to the supper meal except that it persisted. Bang! Bang! Bang! It was incessant. He pointed himself slightly to the right towards the metallic ringing and proceeded cautiously. It was difficult to tell how far he was from the sound so he kept adjusting his direction slightly to better hone in on the source of the reverberating din. The noise became louder and louder and the woods became brighter and brighter until he found himself standing on the edge of the marsh staring at a sign on a barn which said "Payson Blacksmith."

He had walked through most of the night and had gone about a mile away from the home. He had circled and retraced his steps to such a degree that his actual progress had been limited but, as he had never been to this part of Sackville, or rather Westcock, before, it might as well have been a different town, parish and country.

Like a magnet, the constant clanging drew him closer and closer until he was standing in awe at the huge doors of the barn. At first he covered his ears as a huge hammer pounded in time with the ringing as it shaped a glowing yellow horseshoe.

James wasn't the only interested observer. A large work horse stood between crossties looking back casually over a front shoulder. As if to keep the horse's attention, every once in a while the smithy would leave his anvil and, with a pair of tongs that seemed to be part of the molten mass, he would brand the shoe into the bottom of the hoof releasing an acrid smell that burned into James's nose. He didn't mind the smell, it was just different. Eventually satisfied with the overall shape, the man moved over and dunked it all in a barrel as a shrill hiss and poof of white steam rising from the popping water added to the confusion.

Backing into the hind end of the horse, the blacksmith reached under his leather apron between his own legs and grabbed one of the huge hooves. In rapid succession his hand moved from his mouth where he retrieved a square nail, to the animals foot. "Tap, tap, tap." With three swift taps, one to set the nail and two to cause it to disappear, he pounded the fastening home. He repeated these motions several times and then, without a break in rhythm, he grabbed a metal tripod, swung the horse's hoof forward and placed it on this low stand. Trading the hammer for a pair of pliers, he nipped and clinched the protruding points of each nail. Once more he shoved the massive leg forward as he kicked out the tripod, pulled the leg back to the original position between his legs, threw down the hammer and seized a large toothed rasp. However, now the process had the motions of a dance while the file glided over the edge of the hoof spewing white shavings as the tool seemed to float around the foot. This fitting and shaping of the horseshoe to the horse's hoof took less than five minutes and the animal, like James, had been so mesmerized by the whole procedure that neither had moved a muscle.

Only now did Payson stop and wipe the sweat off his brow. A blacksmith does not have to be large in stature and this man proved it. Although he wasn't much taller than James, he probably weighed fifty pounds more. He wore no shirt, only a leather apron over an old pair of wool pants. His body was wiry and the boy noticed the sweat glistening on hard arm and shoulder muscles. Adding to the incongruity of the scene was that instead of being worn and scuffed, his boots were unmarked and shiny with black polish, as if they had just come out of the shoemaker's window.

"Can I help?" James asked tentatively.

The man didn't seem to notice the boy and said nothing. Instead, he led the horse to the back, got another one and repeated the process. These actions continued throughout the morning interrupted only by a customer who came in to pay for some work or to pick up or drop off a horse.

A particularly obstinate creature was leaning his considerable bulk on the blacksmith while he was filing the hoof when, all of a sudden, the man dropped the hoof and stood back. Unbalanced, the horse stumbled amid a great crash of tools and iron shoes ringing on the floor, quickly compensated for this unexpected loss of support and regained his footing. Without a word, Payson went back to work while this horse now stood quietly, holding up his own weight and seemingly embarrassed by the fuss he had caused.

"We used to have horses," James tried again while he moved closer to get a better view of the shoeing. Payson continued to work. As the morning progressed, James began to hand the appropriate tool to Payson much as a nurse assists a doctor. Anticipating the need, he started to add the odd piece of wood or coal to the fire and to pump the bellows to cause the fire to spark and crackle with renewed vigour. Still the blacksmith said nothing.

When the man went back to the stable to exchange animals, the boy swept up the bits and pieces and threw them on the fire, amazed by the way they snapped and glowed. The only clue that Payson realized that the boy was there came after the blacksmith returned from going home for lunch. He shoved a hunk of bread and a piece of cheese towards him told him, "Eat up." To James, it tasted wonderful but the recognition was even better.

Their relationship continued like this for the rest of the day. About the time that the boys and girls would be getting out from school, Payson stopped, hung up his leather apron and doused the fire. He then turned and said, "Clean up here and then come up to the house and the missus will give you something to eat."

James was ecstatic as he regarded this as his first day of work and the meal would be his first pay.

He sat down to rest for a moment and decided that he would just close his eyes for a second. The sounds, the images, the smells of the forest whirled around in his mind mixing with those of the blacksmith shop. Curling up in the straw, he began to breathe more deeply as the fatigue of the last twelve hours caught up with him. His last thoughts in the twilight of wakefulness were of a boat turning over and over and over and beside it was a body rising from the water higher and higher, an arm stretched out above its head. The face was that of John Stevens and in his hand was a filthy boot.

Chapter V

The arrival of morning surprised James. It seemed like mere moments ago that he had decided to rest.

"I thought maybe you had second thoughts about the wife's cooking and reckoned you'd rather be hungry." Payson grinned. He patted his flat belly, "She's really not a bad cook though you wouldn't know it from me. I told her that if you were still here, I'd send you up for breakfast."

This was the most that he had heard Payson say since he had arrived and James took it as some kind of acceptance.

He walked up the hill behind the barn and rapped on the door frame. The white paint was peeling and flaking and James picked at some of it with his fingernail while he waited. Presently a woman who was at least twice the size of the blacksmith ushered him inside where he sat down at a large pine table. She fussed over him until he had eaten a large bowl of warm porridge covered with blueberries and heavy cream and two slabs of the same bread he had enjoyed yesterday except this time they were dripping with honey.

When they weren't otherwise occupied, her hands were constantly wiped on her once white apron.

She bobbed her head with approval at his every bite and kept murmuring, "Eat up. There's more where that came from. You've got to eat to keep strong." It had been a long time since anyone had pestered him in that way and James liked it.

Handing him a basket with lunch provisions in it she admonished, "Now you be sure John brings you up for dinner tonight. Do you like fried chicken?" James smiled.

When he returned to the shop, the smithy was forging a piece of iron for a farm tool while two other men stood by idly. It wasn't clear whether they were watching, waiting or simply putting in time while Payson worked. The blacksmith put his tools down, stowed his lunch for later when he was hungry and looked up at James and said, "I don't have enough work for barely myself here but if you've a mind to, you could take that bay gelding out to the Fawcett place at Four Corners for me. I hear he's in need of someone."

"He's a Methodist so mind he's not converting you," chimed in one of the observers. The other one guffawed choking on a wad of tobacco.

"Watch your cussin' and your swearin' and don't be entertaining him with stories of your whorin' down at Halifax."

The two men bent over, laughing about their jokes at the boy's expense. James never did know what to do when adults behaved like this, so he just looked away and kept his mouth closed.

"If you're not back for supper, I'll know you got a job," Payson called as James led the horse away.

With the horse plodding obediently by his side, he followed the cart path west according to the instructions Payson had given to him. It was amazing that such a large animal, a Clydesdale that could force its will if it so desired, would trudge along so submissively. Despite its massive bulk the horse seemed to prance, enjoying the brisk autumn day as if he were showing off his new shoes and was pleased with the blacksmith's work.

For awhile James crouched down as he led the animal, peaking around the massive neck. "Easy big fella," he soothed. "No pale faces in sight. We'll raid the fort tonight." With a bemused stare, the horse trudged along, continuing to delight in the day.

James began thinking about his situation and he had conflicting feelings for it had been safe and warm at Payson's and the food was good but yet it wasn't home. It wasn't a place where he could settle in and fit in. So, as he walked the road he enjoyed the beauty of the New Brunswick scenery, resplendent with the brilliant changing colours but yet he was conscious that this too was fleeting, as winter would soon invade the Chignecto Valley bringing snow and a harsh, cold and bleak landscape. For the moment, however, he was free.

As the path dipped down closer to the Bay of Fundy, James noticed the dykes, a legacy from the Acadians of the last century who had been driven from their homes by the British Colonials. Arable land was the first and greatest requirement of pioneers in any part of the world and where there were not rocks or cliffs in Canada, there were forests.

James recalled his father telling him, "Farmers hate trees. Sure they use them for building homes, heating and some even sell them, but farmers hate trees because open farmland doesn't just happen, it has to be made to happen."

Trees had to be cut down and the stumps removed before the ground could be hoed or ploughed. Left to rot, the stumps would be around for years so sometimes they burned them and then pulled them out by horse or ox. More commonly, however, crops were planted around the stumps resulting in a yield less than half of what was common in England. Trees were enemies to conquer before land could be farmed.

However James remembered learning in school that there was another way to have land for crops. The early settlers from France were familiar with dykes and reclaiming land from the sea. The Bay of Fundy is famous for the highest tides in the world for the sea floor rises so gradually that in some places the ebb was a mile or more leaving mud flats of rich sediment fortified by decaying vegetation and organisms. In places, some hardy grasses grew close to the shore and twice a day at the low tides, these marshlands were uncovered as the water had receded only to be flooded again at high tides. These salt marshes could be used if the sea could be held back.

Earthen structures, often mixed with soft wood brush, were built like fences. These were about four feet high and were constructed during low tide using the mud from the inside of the dyke, leaving a ditch behind. A dykeing spade which was narrow and quite sturdy, was then used to cut pieces of salt grass, to lift them into place on both sides of the dyke and to tamp them down. The sod helped to keep the earth from eroding.

There was still a problem of how to drain the dykelands of the rain and melting snow. An ingenious, square, box-like conduit was built through the dykes at strategic sites, often where there were existing creek beds. These large wooden pipes or aboiteaux were fitted with one way clapper valves that prevented the salt water from entering the dykeland but, at low tide, permitted the runoff to pour through to the sea.

In a few years the salt had leached out of the soil and crops could be planted. The usual crops were flax, wheat, oats, barley or rye but they grew salt grasses in the marshland on the other side of the dyke and this was prized as winter fodder for the livestock.

At one point James noticed three men working at one of these aboiteaux. They were obviously having some difficulty as the horse, smaller and lighter than Fawcett's Clydesdale, was lathered badly and steamed from exertion as it tried to pull out some of the rotten planks before the tide rose making the job impossible. The men urged on the horse and it struggled bravely, but slipped and skidded in the mud sending chunks of earth and dirt flying in all directions. The men lent their backs to the effort but the result was the same.

They hadn't noticed James so he trotted the big gelding over to where the breathless men stood dirty and fatigued. Rivulets of sweat trickled down their faces marking white lines through the caked filth while large patches of wet had spread under the arms of their shirts and caused their backs to stick to the material. They were exhausted and appeared to be ready to give up.

"Well, William, it looks like help has come just in time," panted one of the men wiping his brow. He rested on his shovel.

The tall, thin man with the gray hair turned to the boy and asked, "Who might you be lad?" The man had a face that appeared humourless although he had kind eyes. They seemed to glint and sparkle as he talked. His gaunt face was tanned a weather-beaten brown with an abundance of wrinkles around his eyes proving that he had worked outside much of his life.

"I am delivering this horse to the Fawcett place. He's stronger than that mare and fresher, too. If we hook him up, I think he can pull those boards out in no time."

"This young boy is ready to take charge," remarked one of the men.

"Won't his owner object to us using his horse?" asked the man they called William.

"I hear he's a religious man," said James, "and I am sure his charity would extend to someone in trouble."

James wasn't sure at all but the prospect of saving the day and, perhaps, landing a coin for his troubles was impossible to resist. A chance to be a hero, this was a young boy's dream.

"Aye," replied William, smiling. "In that case, shall we give it a go, lads?"

Within minutes the spent mare was loosed from her traces and tethered to a nearby tree. The harnesses were quickly slipped on to the gelding and connected back to a stout horizontal wooden pole where a chain was fastened. This chain was wrapped around the planks.

The coolness of the day invigorated the animal and combined with the couple of days rest that he had enjoyed plus the fact that he was doing what he was born to do and what he loved to do, made the Clydesdale impatient to begin the task. He pawed the ground in anticipation. James stood nearby and looked on with awe as the Clydesdale's whole back seemed to lower, the muscles bulging in his shoulders and his hind end. He appeared to dig in as his hooves churned the greasy ground. Muck flew everywhere. There was a creak and a groan followed by a crack and a snap. Mud and ooze sprayed over James as if he were standing in a blizzard with particles of dirt and mire pelting the whole scene. He closed his eyes and raised his arms for protection.

"Watch out there, boy!" someone called.

His world tumbled as he felt a sharp pain and as if some giant had pulled the ground out from underneath him, his feet were swept away. James pitched forward into the slime where he was conscious of the foulest, ugliest stench. He no longer looked or felt like a hero.

His mind raced with terror as he wondered what he had done to create such chaos. What had happened? Then all was quiet. He turned his head and wiped the mud away from his eyes. Looking up he saw the horse and men staring down at him, the broken pieces of board resting at the end of the chain, safely removed from the dyke.

Then, as one, the men began to laugh.

"That will teach the lad to stand too close to King when he gets pulling."

"He's still the strongest horse in these parts."

"Now William, show some charity," one of them quipped, as his eyes squinted with mirth.

A strong hand reached down and pulled James to his feet. The hand belonged to the gray-haired man. Chuckling, he cleaned bits of mud from his clothes and introduced himself, "My name is William Fawcett and I believe that's my horse."

Chapter VI

In a humiliated silence, James helped the men finish the job. Anxious to finish his job and disappear from this place, James trudged up the hill to the Fawcett farm leading the horse to the comfort of his stall. The critical questions and self-doubts flooded back into his awareness as once more he felt that he had squandered an opportunity to impress someone, to do something correctly, and begin a new life. When he had left the blacksmith's shop with high hopes, he had actually believed that it might be this simple, that today he might find both employment and a home. Why had he tried to be a hero with the horse? Why did he say that awful thing about Christian charity? If he had only kept going to the farm, not said anything, not paid any attention to the men and their problem, he could have delivered the horse and then, maybe, gone back to help. Next time he wouldn't be so stupid.

"Stupid, stupid, stupid," he said to himself gritting his teeth as he walked.

William Fawcett watched from the dykes as the boy led the gelding up the path to the farm and he felt badly and was embarrassed with his actions.

"That was unkind of me," he said to his companions. "I shouldn't have teased the lad. He seemed nice enough and certainly not afraid of work."

"You were only funning him."

"I know, but I was looking for somebody to help around the place and he might.... Well, no matter, let's get this finished."

He looked past the boy and saw the farm in the distance. Early in January of 1809, William Fawcett had moved out of his father's house and, with his brother John and his brother-in-law John Dobson, he built that house at Crane's Corners. From a local mill, William had procured the lumber that they would require, as well as the windows and doors and had moved these onto the site the previous summer, in readiness for the winter's work. For days at a time after Christmas, they had lived in a crude hut returning to their homes for more supplies or when the weather became too cold to work or when they wanted a good meal or the company of their families.

The timber for building grew in ready supply and, by utilizing what was nearby, they benefited by clearing the land. Splitting the stones to make the fireplace and chimney proved to be the most difficult chore as the stones were so frozen that the men were unable to crack them without first heating them in a huge fire made of brush. Once assembled into a hearth and chimney, they slathered them with wet mud and left them to harden.

The completed cabin was 20 feet by 15 feet and when he married Sarah Holmes on August 3, 1809, they moved into their own place and although it was crude by today's standards, they were justifiably proud of their new home. William had worked hard to ready the land while Sarah added the feminine touches that the inside of the building required and with the help of willing neighbours, they had added a barn and shed and had been steadily clearing and planting the land.

One fact was very obvious to William. They had done a lot in seven years, however, if they were to make a successful living at farming, they must till more land and to do so, he was going to need some help. Earlier in this year of 1816, he had purchased a twenty-seven acre parcel of land from Israel Thornton who had received it in an original land grant of 1765. As was often the case, Thornton was not actually in the country, for he had returned to the colonies of the south but at the time the temptation to grab some land had been irresistible.

William was forty-six years of age. His mother had died in 1812 and his father, seeming to lose the will to live, died two years later. He was fortunate that his parents had left him sufficient inheritance in money and livestock so that he could build up his own farm, however, he could not do it any more on his own, especially since he now had a young family.

Elizabeth, now six had been born October 24, 1810, and Rufus, now two years old, had been born September 8, 1814. Elizabeth was a delightful child, while it appeared that Rufus tried hard to be just the opposite. Now Sarah was too busy with the family to help him do the farm work.

Meanwhile, when James arrived at the Fawcett home, he was impressed with what he saw for a lot of changes had been made to that original cabin. From the front of the house, it was obvious that the settlers in this new land were not taxed on the number of windows that a residence contained, as they were in Britain.

Inside the barn he was busy cleaning up the big Clydesdale and worked the curry comb in continuous circles while he brushed away the dirt and dander with his other hand. He touched each foot in turn and King obediently raised the hoof to be picked out as Payson had shown him. It was strange that he had worked around horses but had never ridden one, in fact, they frightened him.

His mind kept returning to the scene at the dykes and how he had made a fool of himself. Why couldn't he do anything right? "What an ass I am."

"Did you swear? Who are you?" A small voice startled him back to the present. By the barn door stood a young girl with beautiful, black hair.

Although he ignored the first question, he made the mistake of answering the second and that opened the gates for more and more questions to come tumbling out.

"Why are you brushing King?"

"How did he get so dirty? How did you get so dirty?"

"Do you know my father?"

"Do you go to school? I go to school."

"My name is Elizabeth Fawcett but people call me Betsy. What's your name?"

"I have a brother named Rufus. He cries a lot. Do you have a brother?"

James didn't mind the questions for the little girl was delightful with a sparkle in her eye. His mother would have said that she was "full of beans." She wore a blue frock that was covered with a white apron and she had two matching ribbons in her braided hair except this pretty picture had some flaws. The apron was smudged with dirt, one of the ribbons was dangling undone and one of the braids was threatening to completely untwist. Somehow, all of this just added to her enchantment.

He heard the approach of another person heralded by a young child's crying. His mother would have called it "tired crying" — it was strange that as soon as he was in the presence of a real family, he started thinking of his mother again and the things that she would say.

"I see that you have met Betsy. Is she talking your ear off?" The woman who had a young boy in her arms shushed and rocked as she talked. There was an evident family resemblance between the mother and the daughter, each with the same raven hair, but James was unable to see many distinguishable traits in the scrunched up red face of the bawling boy.

"Yes ma'am. I mean, no ma'am." Why did he find talking to adults so difficult? "I mean, yes, I have met her but no, she isn't bothering me."

"His name is James George and he is bringing King back and he met father and he's cleaning him up before he goes in his stall. You know what? He's looking for work and he doesn't go to school and he has no mother and father."

"Well, Elizabeth, it seems you know all about James George and it appears, as usual, you will tell the whole parish."

"James, will you have some apple cider with us before you leave? We don't get to see a lot of strangers around here. It is about time for this wee one's nap so come up to the house when you are done here. I think that I can find a cookie or two."

She turned and left with the two children as James cleaned up and put the horse in his stall.

Had Mrs. Fawcett or Betsy remained there or waited for him, he probably would have gone up to the house for the cider. Still embarrassed about the incident with Mr. Fawcett, he quietly slipped out of the barn and turned to go back to town. Judging from the light he would just have time to make it back for some of Mrs. Payson's fried chicken.

On the long walk back he mulled over all that he had seen, all that had transpired today. It seemed that just as things start to go well, something bad happens. This had been the pattern of his life. He brooded about whether it was just cruel fate that caused this or if he was doing something wrong. Had he somehow offended God and, therefore, He was punishing him? By fighting in the boat, he had caused their death and now he was doomed forever. He recalled his mother once telling him that God never gives us more to bear than we are able to handle, but even that memory didn't ease his pain.

The gloom and guilt that he was harbouring were far more weighty than a thirteen-year-old should have had to carry. He had experienced more in his short years than some face in a lifetime. Surely he couldn't be asked to bear more. What would he do now? Where would he go? It was getting colder outside and maybe he should just lie here by the side of the road. "Who would know? Who would care anyway?" he said aloud.

It was starting to rain. "What a perfect end to a perfect day," he muttered bitterly. His dark thoughts and self-pitying reflections consumed his attention to such a degree that he didn't hear the horse and cart approach him from behind.

"Lad, wait up a minute. I want to talk to you."

Startled, James turned around. It was Mr. Fawcett with Elizabeth on the seat beside him. What had he done now? Had he not put King away safely? He was too tired, too discouraged to even care.

"You left without tasting Sarah's apple cider. Look, all I have heard from this little one is 'James this' and 'James that.' I didn't get a chance to thank you properly for your help today and we would be pleased if you would stay for supper. I won't get any peace unless you do."

"Please say, yes, James," chimed in Elizabeth.

Numbly, James climbed into the wagon and grinned. He thought, "Maybe my luck is beginning to change."

Chapter VII

As James returned to the Fawcett farm and sat down for his meal with them, he felt a little awkward but each member on the family soon made him feel at home. He soon realized that they expected or required nothing of him except to listen and to eat.

He glanced admiringly around the inside of their home; this log cabin with the chimney and fireplace was pure luxury compared to the typical shanty. Wood planking had replaced the usual dirt floor and real doors were used instead of hanging skins. The logs were pine and here and there sap still seeped from exposed knots. The cracks in the logs were chinked with a mixture of lime, mud, moss and sand which provided an effective barrier to the wind, rain and snow. The real glass in the windows screamed to James that this family was well off.

A large pine table dominated the furniture with enough spool chairs for six people. James had never before seen a fireplace with two ovens and, according to Elizabeth, one was used for baking bread. In one corner a large spinning wheel waited to turn the flax and wool into yarn. However, what caught his attention was the two stuffed chairs and the settee which looked so comfortable.

They all sat down together for dinner and William said grace. He thanked James for his work on the dyke and apologized for remaining silent about the horse. "Lad, it was not 'charitable' of me to tease you so," his eyes twinkling as he passed him a heaping bowl of Sarah's stew. "You did right in bringing the horse to our aid. The land is harsh and we must all stick together if any of us are to survive and improve our lot."

"I know that William wouldn't willfully offend any one, James." Sarah watched approvingly as the boy shoveled in bits of beef, potato, carrot and onion, smothered in a rich brown gravy. "He was very appreciative of your help today and it sounds like you arrived just in the nick of time. I am sorry that you got so dirty down at the dykes. Elizabeth, pass the bread to James."

Elizabeth did as she was told. It was obvious that she had been coached not to interrupt adult conversations and it was just as obvious that to comply was causing her no end of anguish; she was bursting to join in the talk.

James took a mouth-shaped hunk out of the thick slab of brown bread which he had covered with creamy white butter.

"You know that just because the crops are in, the work doesn't stop on a farm. With winter coming there is plenty to keep us busy until the planting," continued William, his spoon poised in mid air. "With the additional land, we have many trees to fell once the snow is here for they are easier to move around once there is a blanket of snow on the ground. I would like to get the front field ploughed before it freezes as that way the ice and frost can do their work and break down the dirt clods for spring. Elizabeth, get the boy another glass of milk."

He chased the stew and bread with great swallows of the warm, thick milk.

Sarah carried on, "I used to be able to work out in the fields with William, but lately the demands of the children have restricted my work to around the house." Her gaze went to young Rufus who, sensing that it was he who was limiting his mother, promptly stuck out his tongue at James, letting half-chewed food slide down his chin. He followed this up with an idiotic grin.

William, leaning towards James, picked up the conversation, "You know, a lot of people think that farming is contemptible as are we who engage in this sort of work. I know that we who struggle with the soil are mocked and ridiculed by the fishermen and lumbermen, but it is a necessary and important work that we do." He smiled slightly. "Of course, the only one lower is a farm labourer."

James reached under the table and held Rufus's foot which had been kicking him incessantly during the meal.

The passion coloured William's speech, as he persevered. "There are new methods being tried and new kinds of animal husbandry and crop cultivation that, although accepted in other areas, are only just becoming tried in these parts. You know the legacy that the Acadians left us wasn't all positive."

It was obvious that he was just getting warmed up to the subject which was fine with James as he was content to just listen since he had his mouth engaged in more important pursuits. "On the one hand, the elaborate dykes allowed for land to be used for crops without the clearing of trees and this land was rich in nutrients from millions of years of decaying organisms and, unlike the soil of the highlands, it seems to have the ability to sustain yield for an indefinite period of time without manure."

Sarah refilled the boy's bowl while William pushed his aside, put down his utensil and persisted. "On the other hand, this encouraged the neglect of proper farming methods, which others ridicule as 'book farming'. They say that if the old methods were good enough for their parents in Normandy, they would be good enough here in this new land. Of course none of them admit that any progress was happening at home. This adoption of sloppy agricultural practices means that much of our land is under half tillage so that the labour of planting and harvesting has to be spread over twice the area to provide the same amount of yield."

Sarah cleared the empty bowls and replaced them with plates of pudding made from apples, brown sugar and oatmeal. She smothered this with a heavy cream poured from a painted china pitcher. James could not remember when he had tasted anything any better.

William hardly paused for dessert. "Moreover, since their efforts were not needed to improve or work the land, there are very few real farmers. Most augment what money they make by trapping and trading in furs, or by fishing or by lumbering. This sloppy method of farming is shown in the care and husbandry of their animals." Wiping his mouth, he pushed back his chair. "Rather than winter over their herds, they often slaughter them in the fall and start all over in the spring which does little to improve the breeds. As manure isn't required for improving the soil it isn't used and is simply allowed to build up in the stalls and barns, with the question becoming how to get rid of it instead of employing it productively."

"William wants to start an association of farmers in the area. They can buy things together as well as discuss new ideas." Sarah paused to clean Rufus's face and gather up the bits of food that surrounded his place. "I know the baby can be annoying but I am a good cook and Elizabeth adores you. We have plenty of room."

"So what do you say, lad?"

James was conscious of four pairs of eyes riveted on him waiting for an answer. The only problem was, he wasn't sure of the question. "I, ah, am not sure that I understand all that stuff you were talking about but it sure was a delicious meal, sir. I can't remember when I ate so much, ma'am. Thank you very much."

Finally Elizabeth who had contained herself all through the meal, exploded, "But will you stay. Will you live with us here and help us on the farm?"

James was speechless. Even if he hadn't been so intent on the excellent food, it is doubtful that he would have discerned what William Fawcett had been asking him throughout the meal.

"I can give you room and board and will pay you a half a pound a week." William paused. "Your wages will start immediately and no half pay during the winter months like some of the other farmers."

"You can have Rufus's room. He sleeps with us anyway."

Elizabeth screamed, "Say yes, James, say yes."

"Sure," said James. The tears welled up in his eyes again, but this time they were a different kind of tears. A family, a home, a job — maybe there really was a God.

William went to get the night's wood for the fire while Sarah cleared up the kitchen area. Elizabeth got ready for bed and it was only Rufus and James sitting at the table. James took one last spoonful of the rich dessert and turned to Rufus. Surely this little fellow couldn't be that bad. After checking that no one else was watching he opened his mouth wide giving Rufus a good view of the partially chewed pudding. Rufus cried.

Chapter VIII

Preparing for winter filled the next few weeks. James settled in to his new life very easily and was enjoying the Fawcett family. He still found Rufus a little hard to take but avoided him whenever possible and made certain allowances when he observed how much the family loved the two year old.

James had never had a younger brother and so living with one so young was a new experience for him but he found Rufus a very demanding child, always wanting, no, always requiring, his mother's attention. From the moment he woke up the chant "I want" echoed through the house. Nothing anyone seemed to do for the young boy was ever enough as it seemed that, to him, it was all a game to command and demand. Yet he never seemed to be happy or content.

On one occasion, when his grandparents, Mr. and Mrs. Holmes, came to visit, they brought Rufus a toy top and Elizabeth a cornhusk doll. They had purchased the top from a store during a trip to Halifax while a local neighbour had made the doll. The boy was not satisfied until he had dropped the top down the well and dismantled the doll, husk by husk.

James's impressions of William Fawcett changed radically since he had first met him at the dykes. William was a quiet, mild man who appeared to be universally respected through the county. Neighbours or members of the church would come by in the evening to talk with him or ask his opinion. John, William's older brother, was a frequent visitor and they often huddled by the fire discussing the affairs of the church or the politics of the day.

William was very good to James and the two worked along side each other, often without speaking for hours. He never expected the boy to do any job that he would not do himself, nor did he keep the more enjoyable jobs and delegate the less pleasurable ones. He exhibited the utmost faith in James and his abilities and never pushed him into something that was too difficult. Yet James seemed to flourish physically and in self-confidence, the former because of Sarah's cooking and the latter do to William's trust and encouragement.

One afternoon as they were chopping and splitting wood, William stopped and gazed intently at the horizon and said, "Lad, we are in for a whale of a storm. See the way those clouds are forming up like an anvil? That's a sure sign and, besides, I can feel it in my bones. I wouldn't be surprised if we had snow. The cattle are down on the marsh and they won't come up until milking time. Take King and collect them."

James sucked in his breath and felt a twinge of the old uncertainty creep into the pit of his stomach. William didn't know about his fear of horses. What if he couldn't do it? What if he let Mr. Fawcett down? What if he failed again?

Before he could protest William added, "I know you can do it and I am counting on you. I am taking the mare and wagon to go and collect Sarah and the children. They're down at John's."

As James entered the barn, King seemed to know that there was a job for him and he began to bounce and prance about his stall impatiently. Leading him out by the halter, James put him in the crossties and grabbed the bridle from the peg on the wall. He stood on the milking stool beside the great Clydesdale's head, holding the bridle the way he had seen it done before. He did not relish the thought of sticking his hand in the behemoth's mouth and wondered how he would ever get King to take the bit, but, as he raised his hand, the horse lowered his head and nuzzling the bit seemed to suck it into place without James doing a thing.

James gathered the reins and led the horse outside the barn. King was so invigorated by the cool air, the impending storm and the prospect of an adventure that he lifted his feathered feet up high as he danced around. Being mindful of the massive hooves, James moved him over to the chopping block.

"Easy King. Relax big fella. It's me. Easy now. We've got to do this," he pleaded with the horse.

He was unsure how he would ever mount King but as he gathered the reins and a handful of mane in his left hand and swung his right leg up and over the massive back, the animal stood very still. A horseman would say that the beast sensed his rider and compensated for his lack of experience. Whatever the reason, King swung around and, without any guidance from James, he trotted down the path to the marsh. The boy simply hung on to the mane with both hands and tried desperately not to get bounced off.

Once the cows saw the horse and rider approaching they stirred and, deciding it must be milking time, they assembled, formed up and waited to be led home. King swung around in a large arc, seemed to wait until the cows were formed up and guided the procession to safety. James felt particularly proud as he slipped off the great gelding, put him in his stall and safely penned the cows. He had conquered his fear and had saved the day. He suspected that the horse may have had some knowledge of the proper procedure, even if he didn't and this fact was reinforced by Elizabeth telling him later, "Usually father asks me to take King and get the cows, but I don't mind. When I'm not here you can do it."

Trees that are planted for fruit will not do well for many years and sometimes farmers must wait decades to harvest the results of their planting. One of the exceptions is the apple tree that flourished in the soil and climate of New Brunswick. Fawcett farm had been planted with over an acre of apple trees that provided a copious bounty by the fifth year after planting. Sarah used these in every way possible. They had apples for snacking, apple desserts including pies, dumplings, puddings, cakes, crumbles, pastries, breads, cookies, fritters, tarts, sauce, tortes and the family favourite, baked apples with maple syrup and stiff cream. She dried some apples and put them away in long strings to last them through the winter. Carefully, she stored bushels of the unblemished ones in the root cellar which gave them fresh apples well into the new year. They washed the grounders and squeezed and drank the juice or fermented it into cider. To eliminate any worms, they boiled the really bad ones and slopped them to the pigs. Still there were more apples than they could possibly use so these were traded with the neighbours for other food or services.

One of the tasks in preparation for winter was the slaughter of some of the animals that would not be used for breeding next spring. Often the neighbours would gather to help and share in the meat. An experience to remember, not because of its brutality for everyone accepted this part of farm life, but because of its adventure, butchering day was something special to break up the sameness of the routine and brought with it the promise of an exceptional meal once the day's activities were done.

"James, you and the boys get a bonfire started in the corner of the yard and hang that huge kettle of water above it. We'll see if we can't rope the hind legs of one of these hogs."

By the time that the water was boiling, William had done his job. This was not always an easy task and could end in injury if they were not careful for the pigs were fast and did not want to be caught and, as usual, the ground was muddy. They threw the other end of the rope over the limb of a stout tree and with James's help pulled the pig up in the air. The squealing was shrill, sharp and prolonged and James had never heard the equal. With the pig killed and the blood drained, they plunged the carcass into the boiling water so that they could remove the hair more easily.

Two neighbours who were obviously experts took over as they attacked the carcass with sharp knives. They saved the liver and then began cutting up the pieces. In a few minutes instead of a pig, there were hams, shoulders, bacon, spare ribs, chops, steaks and roasts, with every part used. The head was made into headcheese and the fat was rendered to lard, the feet were pickled for pig's knuckles which Sarah said was a delicacy, the hams went to a small smoke house behind the barn to cure over a smoldering hickory fire or age in a salty brine. Sarah leaned several racks of the ribs against a log next to the fire where they roasted a toasty brown under her watchful eye. With eager anticipation the children checked these often as the tantalizing aroma beckoned and teased them until finally they were allowed to attack and devour them.

"Watch this!" yelled William and tossed the ears to the dogs who fought among themselves to see who got the largest piece. Then they ran around, unsuccessfully looking for a quiet place to eat the trophy in peace. "Just like our children," he observed.

"Oh, I don't eat ears," Elizabeth announced and everyone laughed.

William had a favourite saying which he repeated whenever a hog was butchered. "Nothing is wasted on the Fawcett farm. Everything is used except the squeal."

Sarah would always add, "If you've ever heard Uncle Henry's fiddle playing, you'd think that the squeal was used, too." James mused to himself that, on a good day, Rufus could give either the pigs or Uncle Henry a run for their money.

William related an interesting tale that last year they had all gone over to the Tolar Thompson place on the edge of the marsh to butcher some hogs. There was an unused well that seemed to be ideal for hanging the hogs while they were slaughtered as they could wind them up on the mechanism that had been once used for raising the bucket. The doomed animal kicked and squealed with the usual vigour, rocking the wooden supports which held the crank but this banging and smashing disturbed the ground to such an extent that more snakes than anyone had ever seen emerged from the wooden sides of the well. The violent motion caused by the pig had disturbed several nests of these harmless reptiles who fled for safer homes. William added, "That was one time when the noise of the dying hog wasn't the loudest noise. The screams of the women and children drowned it out."

When it came time to butcher the cattle and the sheep, William announced a change. "I have arranged with Charles Bulmer to purchase a two year old ox in the spring. In exchange we are going to give him six sheep, two to be butchered for mutton. Today we will drive them down to the pond by the marsh."

The two dogs warmed to their task and nipped at the heels of the fated creatures as they drove them down to the lower pond. There they forced them into an ever-narrowing fenced path that eventually only became wide enough for one animal at a time. One at a time they were made to enter the cold pond where William and James washed their coats free of the dirt that they had collected since summer as a neighbour grabbed the newly cleaned animal and worked a pair of shears while holding the sheep between his legs. James marveled at the skill of the man as he seemed to roll the wool off the animal in one large piece. Hating water and particularly with it being so cold this time of year, the sheep scampered up the opposite bank looking every bit like skinned cats.

"Samuel, leave the wool on these last two a little longer if you please. They are the ones up for butchering."

He removed the hides from these animals and they processed them in the usual fashion. It occurred to James that for such a large animal you ended up with a lot of wool but not very much meat. William explained that the wool was carded and combed before spinning it into a coarse yarn that could be knit or turned into homespun wool cloth. Salt was poured over the two hides before they were hung to cure.

Bees of any kind, for any reason were very popular in the farming communities. Barn raisings, quilting bees, harvesting bees, whatever the reason, neighbours would gather to give a hand with some of the more arduous jobs. These boring tasks that were so time-consuming became fun, almost like a game, when they shared the work. They also provided an opportunity for socializing and having a banquet. Shortly after James's arrival, the Fawcetts went over to the Ryan farm for a corn-husking bee where the women and younger children sat and husked the corn to be stored as winter feed while the men, soon bored with the gossip and talk, began pitching horseshoes at an iron stake.

The boys gathered and introduced James to a game called peewee, where they hit a short stick with a larger stick from a circle drawn in the ground. To James, the rules were complicated and seemed to grow and change to fit the situations or disputes as they arose, resulting in some of the older and more skillful players always managing to win.

A corn roast was the highlight of the day with unhusked ears of sweet corn being dug out of the embers of a fire pit and eaten with fresh, unsalted butter.

The days were getting shorter and as a consequence more time was spent indoors. With little chance to accomplish anything worthwhile outside after supper, each was busy inside in his own way. They put down preserves and winter food supplies, split wood and kindling, and readied the flax and wool for spinning. Soon a light blanket of snow would be covering what had been fields of hay and wheat and corn, and Christmas would be here; many preparations still remained.

Chapter IX

The days before Christmas were very busy so William and James limited their work around the farm to only the maintenance chores; the animals were fed and the stalls and barn were cleaned out as usual, but any projects and extra jobs were put on hold as everyone assisted with the festive preparations. For more than a week before the twenty-fifth, neighbours, friends and relatives dropped in for a friendly greeting and a cup of Sarah's pungent mulled cider which was kept warming over the fire all day. The smell of cloves and cinnamon permeated the house and mingled with the sweet aromas of baked goods which emerged from the oven more and more frequently as the day drew closer.

One morning during this pre-Christmas week, William started to dress in his heavy coat and turned to Sarah and said, "I think that it would not be out of place to give the lad his present a few days earlier than is the custom."

Sarah beamed and retrieved a bulky bundle from the other room which she placed proudly in James's arms. He immediately recognized the hides from the two sheep that they had butchered earlier, except their shape had been altered. By careful sewing and cutting, Sarah had fashioned the pelts into a long coat with the wool side, cut short, on the inside, while she had oiled and softened the skin on the outside to a wonderful bronze colour. There were no arms, pockets, or fasteners but as soon as he slipped it on James could feel the softness and warmth of the wool next to his shirt. He wouldn't have been prouder if she had given him the finest silk topcoat.

"We figured that Rufus could wear it once you are finished with it and furthermore, you can't go out to get a Christmas tree in this cold without proper clothing."

Having never heard of this custom, Sarah explained that people in France decorated an evergreen and the Acadians had introduced this habit in the area. Although not yet customary in Britain, many of the settlers around here were following this tradition. Just as the Dutch settlers had continued to give gifts on Christmas Eve as they did in Holland, this culture embraced many new ideas and fashions.

After hitching up King to the stone boat and perching Elizabeth on his broad back, they headed back into the woods. The stone boat was a flat boat built of plank and used to haul stone and other heavy objects over the rough ground. Where a cart or wagon required a smoother path, the stone boat glided over the rocks and stumps and uneven terrain. Often filled with rocks and stones when clearing the land, it was particularly useful in winter or even over the wet marshland.

"King isn't really the right animal for pulling one of these which is why we are getting an ox in the spring. You see," continued William, "when a horse gets stuck in the soft ground it will rear up and dance around, while an ox puts its full strength into the load. You'll see when we get the new animal."

Picking out a suitable Christmas tree was not an easy job. Pines that looked just fine from a distance, displayed bare sections when they were examined more closely. Others were rejected as being too large or too small. Trunks were often twisted or bent from the wind. Elizabeth was getting cold and what started as a pleasurable adventure was no longer fun.

"Just be thankful that young Rufus isn't with us," commented William. "Let's go back to that first one that we all liked. It wasn't that bad."

A few strokes from his keen ax felled the tree and they loaded it on the stone boat for the trek back to the house. The ride was bumpy and even King was eager to return to the warmth and comfort of his stall so, as William urged him on, they crashed and jolted over the snow, losing their load on more than one occasion.

With the tree propped up in the corner of the main room, they placed bird nests that they had found on the branches and twisted coloured bits of material punctuated with bows of brightly dyed yarn around and around the tree. Sarah and Elizabeth had strung some red berries from a bush in the woods to create a pleasing garland which drooped and looped among the greenery while they completed the pleasing effect with a few sprigs of sumac berries .

The family sat back and admired their creation and drank mugs of hot milk sweetened with maple syrup. To James, it was like a dream to be sharing this season with this family and he only hoped that he would not wake up and find himself back at the home. His memories of his parents were becoming dimmer and sometimes several days passed without his thinking of the awful tragedy and without his blaming himself for their deaths. Sarah and William were treating him as part of the family and he no longer felt like a hired hand.

He adored Elizabeth and, although he pretended otherwise, he relished the times when she would climb into his lap and ask him to read to her or tell her a story. Her long black hair, soft against his face, she would snuggle into him and wrap her small arms around his neck. Often she would say nothing and, for James, these were his favourite times.

Rufus continued to be an unhappy little boy who was mean and spiteful. It seemed to James that everyone avoided him and his moods as much as possible because when he wasn't unhappy he was finding ways to make others unhappy. Even the farm dogs and barn cats knew him well enough to run the other way to avoid having him pull an ear or a tail. One day James overheard a farm hand at the Thompson place say, "Every once 'awhile I see'd a cull like that born 'cept on the farm we drown 'im."

Christmas Eve was a special evening. Their evening meal was taken earlier than normal and consisted of a particularly delicious meat pie that was made with equal amounts of pork, beef and venison, chopped finely and mixed with onion, potatoes and turnip. Enveloped in a golden crust, it was served piping hot with sufficient for seconds and thirds. Sarah said that the recipe came from some French neighbours. It seemed to James that the atmosphere was calmer than normal around the Fawcett table with Rufus taking a respite from his typical fussing.

They washed the dishes and completed the clean up in record time and then built up the fire to a sparkling brightness. As was becoming the custom, William sat in the large chair to the right of the fireplace while James relaxed in the smaller chair opposite him, Rufus played on the rag rug between them while, settled in the settee, Sarah and Elizabeth gazed into the flames.

William read from the Bible which had been given to the Fawcett family by John Wesley when they left Yorkshire on *The Two Friends* in 1774. James was familiar with the story of the baby Jesus being born in the stable in Bethlehem, having heard it in church and from his mother however, before this particular Christmas Eve, he had never understood the beauty and the serenity of the tale. As they sat by the fire, the bright patches and shadows dancing across their faces, he thought of how fortunate Mary and Joseph were to have found a safe haven on that faraway farm and how lucky the baby was to be wanted and loved. He felt just as fortunate this Christmas Eve as he mused how a twist of fate could change a life forever. He prayed that nothing would happen to disturb this family and their quiet existence for James was experiencing the peace and tenderness of Christmas that year.

As the children were finally growing restless, James said, "I have a little something for Elizabeth and Rufus when you are ready for bed. It is under your pillows."

The transition was accomplished in record time without their parents giving too much attention to scrubbing the stubborn spots behind their ears. The first to his bed, Rufus turned over his pillow to reveal a whistle that James had made for him.

Remembering exactly how his father had done the same for him in days gone by, James had selected a straight piece of green poplar growing by the marsh, about as big around as his thumb and six inches in length. Now was the tricky part. He had slit the bark the length of the twig and slowly and methodically worked at it until, still intact, it was loosened from the wood. Painstakingly, he had carved a tiny groove in the length of the wood and then a larger aperture for the mouth.

Now by blowing softly and moving the bark back and forth along the stem, Rufus could produce a noise variable in pitch which modulated between a high, piercing whistle and a low, haunting warble. Many times in the next few days, the family would wonder, sometimes aloud, if it were the best choice of presents for Rufus but, as his father remarked, "At least when he's blowing, he's not crying and probably not getting in trouble."

Elizabeth carefully moved her pillow to reveal her present, a piece of paper, folded up in a little packet and tied with a length of pink ribbon. Her tiny fingers eagerly tugged at the bow. She unfolded each section of the paper to reveal a four leaf clover which had been pressed and coated with wax.

"I hunted especially for it," James remarked. "They say it's a good luck charm."

"Oh, James. I'll treasure it forever. It will be my most favourite thing." With that Elizabeth gave him a kiss and a hug.

Sarah exclaimed, "It was good luck when you came to live with us." They all agreed.

The young children safely in bed, they sat by the fire drinking a cup of tea and munching on some sweet shortbread. There was a kindness in Sarah's voice as she said, "You know that was very thoughtful of you. You are very kind to the children."

"I have something for you two, as well." James revealed a small plaque made from a piece of board which he had stained dark with some boot polish. On it he had carved the following verse:

"Of all the crops a man can raise,
Or stock that he employs,
None yields such profit and such praise
As a crop of Girls and Boys."

"That will find a favourite spot above the mantle of the fireplace," laughed William, "though I fear it might be a mite bit late for growing any more of those crops."

"We have a little something for you." Sarah smiled. "William says that you are always borrowing his. We hope you like it." She handed James a new two-bladed pocket knife, made of fine Sheffield steel encased in a rippled piece of carved deer antler.

Her husband added, "It's a good one. You must keep it sharpened. You know a dull blade is more dangerous than a sharp one."

"I know," said James, the tears running down his face. "I know."

Christmas Day started out the same as any other day on the farm with the chores to be done however, it didn't take the animals long to realize that something was different as the morning feed was a bran mash. In a large bucket, William moistened cracked bran with hot water from the kettle on the fire and after it was stirred to the consistency of a dry porridge, he added corn kernels, bits of apple, slices of carrot and a generous scoop of oats. King's whinny greeted them at the barn door and James watched how he nosed through the steaming mixture picking out bits and pieces that met his fancy. He was very gentle and refined for such a powerful horse.

"Sarah will have something special for our breakfast this morning," William remarked. "I think we are in for a treat of fried fat pork and eggs this morning before we go to church." So they hurried up to the house for breakfast.

Later, as they glided along the snow-covered path in the red cutter, Sarah and the two young ones bundled under blankets in the back, while James rode up front with William. Handing James the reins, he said, "You take over. King knows the way if you have forgotten." Bells which had been added to the harness jangled and combined with the clopping sound of horse hooves to produce an altogether magical ride that morning so that as they looked out over the steamy marshes to the gray bay and the snow began filtering down very finely, each was thinking special private thoughts.

James marveled at how happy he had been lately scarcely wanting to believe his own luck. William reflected on the changes that had transpired over the last year and was thankful. Sarah pondered the love that she had for the people in that sleigh and the love that she felt in return. Elizabeth clutched her little Bible in her white gloved hands and drank in the beauty of the scene checking between the pages of the book to ensure that the four leaf clover was still safe. Rufus wondered about the possibility of another piece of hard candy if he began to make a fuss.

The service held in the Methodist meeting house about a mile and a half from home, was elongated by the joyous singing of many hymns, the most notable of which was "Hark, The Herald Angels Sing" written by John Wesley's brother, Charles. Known as the poet of the Methodist movement, Charles had written over seven thousand hymns, and it seemed to James as if they sang most of them this day. He didn't mind, however, as he loved the singing. Of the whole congregation, no one had a more beautiful singing voice than William's brother, John. Impressive in height, he would lead the congregation with his massive voice belting out the words for all to hear so that one old man remarked after the service, "Such a voice I'll ne'er hear again, till the music up yonder."

If visiting was one of the common pastimes of the day, it was particularly well-observed this day with company coming and going while Sarah greeted each one with something delicious to eat and drink. James kept the cider cups filled while Elizabeth passed the pretty plate of goodies.

William's brother, John, and his family came over later in the afternoon. George, the eldest son, aged eighteen, sat with the men by the fire while Sarah and Elleanor, John's wife, were busy with the dinner preparations. Little Eleanor and Elizabeth, both about the same age, went off to play with their dolls. Will, who was also thirteen, was motioning to James.

"Let's go down to the barn before we get saddled with looking after Rufus."

That job, however, fell to Anne who was almost fourteen and was already showing the signs of developing into a beautiful young woman. James couldn't take his eyes off her and she seemed to notice him as well. She filled out her dress particularly well and, on more than one occasion, she caught him staring at her shapely body. This didn't seem to bother

her as she was very comfortable with her development and she was amused by his attention. He loved the way her mouth curled up at the corners when she smiled at him but James had little experience with girls and found himself tongue-tied whenever he was alone with her so most of the time he simply looked, not having the nerve to talk.

Finally Will, who had witnessed James's odd behaviour, dragged him off to the barn where they played up in the loft.

"Grab this rope and we'll swing out over the animals. See who can get lower." They rigged a rope and swung out over the stalls below, daring each other to go lower and try to touch the animals' backs. They took turns trying the new knife, which they both agreed was a beauty.

James liked Will and they had sought each other out at the many family functions as they both seemed to enjoy the same things. When the two were playing, though, others had to be wary of the pranks and plots which they constantly hatched. Although they both got blamed for escapades gone awry, most credited Will as the brains behind the schemes.

Dinner was magnificent with a roast suckling pig, complete with apple in his mouth, and a golden brown goose as the major attractions. Vegetables and preserves overflowed the table and plates were heaped again and again until everyone was stuffed. James listened to the happy mingling of all the voices as several conversations competed for importance but, whenever he could, he shot an admiring glance in Anne's direction. This first Christmas with the Fawcetts was a joyous occasion.

After trying the various pies and puddings, James jumped to his feet, eager to help with the clearing of the dishes.

Noticing his assistance, Sarah remarked, "Well, you are a big help tonight."

"James is sweet on Anne," shouted Elizabeth.

"He's been silly around her all day," added Eleanor.

James looked down in flushed embarrassment as Anne responded, "He has not. He's just being sweet. Maybe Will could learn a few manners from him. Besides everybody knows that Isaac Goodwin is my boyfriend."

James didn't know.

The elder William chipped in, "Ah yes, but Baie Verte is a ways away. Out of sight, out of mind."

"True, uncle," replied Anne, "but absence makes the heart grow fonder."

It took older brother George to put an end to the quips. "I always figured that not in my arms, in somebody else's."

The good-natured banter had deflected the attention away from James for which he was grateful. In a way, he hadn't minded the teasing for being in a large group like this reminded him of happy times when he, too, had been part of a family.

As James lay in bed that night, he clutched his new knife and reflected on the wonderful day. All was quiet save the muted voices of William and Sarah from the fireside.

"What were you and Johnnie talking about all day?"

"We were discussing the year's successes. He also mentioned that there has been some talk that some of the congregation want a meeting house at Crane's Corners. They feel it is too far to go to the north for services. Johnnie feels that we should have a church in our own community."

"Dear, what do you think?"

William mused, "Ah, well, I am afraid that it will too soon happen. I only hope and pray that it isn't the wedge that splits us Methodists apart." He furrowed his brow and appeared concerned. "It will be a shame to worship separate from our northern brethren."

Tired, satiated, and satisfied, James drifted asleep. It was probably fate that prevented him from hearing the rest of the conversation.

William looked even more troubled. "Johnnie also expressed concern that we have accepted James so much into our home and, in his words, we are not treating him at all like a hired hand."

"He is your older brother, William, and I respect him however, he does willingly share his opinions with anyone who will listen and, indeed, with those who won't. Again, how do you feel?"

"I like James. He is amiable, hard-working, industrious. In a lot of circumstances he evidences the traits that I hope and pray our own son, Rufus, will exhibit. Bringing this boy into our home was not wrong." William smiled at Sarah. "He has done credit to our decision and in a lot of ways I think we have provided the stability and family that he so desires."

"I agree, dear. I feel sympathy for his plight and yet pity is not what he desires." Looking lovingly at her husband Sarah added, "Johnnie thinks a good deal, he reads ravenously and he writes daily in that journal, I suppose it is only natural that he would share his thoughts. I guess that is why some call him John, the Critic."

William and Sarah sat a little longer in front of the fire, neither wanting to disturb the enchantment of the moment, the magic of the day.

Chapter X

The enchanting Christmas season gave way to boring days of white and gray that reeked a sameness; the beauty of the winter was now commonplace and the activities around the farm mirrored the tableau. As they watched the snow drift down, they wondered if there would ever be an end to the cold, bleak days that yeilded so quickly to the darkness of nights.

Clearing trees was the everyday routine and after the usual chores and jobs around the barn, any spare moment was spent logging. One day seemed much like the next — chop the trees, trim the branches, pile and burn them. King, steaming and snorting in the frigid air, was connected by a length of chain to the trunks and was forced to pull and plod through the snow, along worn paths in the whiteness to an area beside the house. Here William and James cut the hardwood into fireplace sized logs or stacked the lengths of pine for a future trip to the mill. This being completed, they turned around, headed out to the field and repeated the process again and again and again. Meals, toilet breaks, very bad weather, cups of scalding tea, broken tools or machinery or dull axes were all welcome as they broke the monotony of the work.

As James got dressed one morning to begin the drudgery, William put his hand on his shoulder and stopped him. "Not today, lad. We have a good start on the winter's work and it's time we took you hunting. We both need a break and it might give Sarah a little variety for our dinners."

With that he went over to the locked chest and, opening the door, he motioned to James to join him. "I am particular about the guns and I will show you how I like things kept."

He explained that the chest was always locked with the key hanging high on a hook beside the fireplace. The three rifles were nestled in slots, each carved to hold a particular one with its breach in a safe, opened position. Wooden boxes of unopened ammunition were stacked neatly in one corner and the oily rags and cleaning equipment attested to the care that was taken of these weapons.

"See this block." William held up a solid block of wood with 25 identical little holes bored in it, each about the size of a baby finger. "When we open a box of slugs, we put them in the holes. We take what we need for the hunt and after our return, we replace the empty holes with either unused slugs or the spent brasses so every hole should be filled. This way we will be safe knowing that there is no live ammunition about and, also, we will have the casings ready for refilling."

By now, James was familiar with William's neatness and his insistence that everything be kept in its place, however, he sensed the extra special care and attention devoted to the firearms and adopted a similar attitude. William removed two rifles and, placing a handful of slugs into each of two leather bags, he slung one over his shoulder and gave the other to James.

As with most boys his age in New Brunswick, James was familiar with guns and had experience shooting. Since his father was an army officer, there had been plenty of opportunities to care for and shoot a rifle properly.

However, unlike his pals, his father had never taken him deer hunting. His older brother, Peter, had been allowed but James's age and Mrs. Anderson's over-protecting nature conspired to prevent his going. He was excited about this new adventure.

"We are heading into the northwest woods. I saw some fresh scrapes there. We will be back by supper."

Sarah handed them each some lunch wrapped in a coloured handkerchief and bade them to be careful. As they headed towards the woods, they sent the dogs back to the house with some angry words and a few thrown pieces of frozen dirt.

"With the snow up to our knees like this, we should consider making some snowshoes. The Indians make them and they are a wood frame with a lattice in them that allows you to walk on top of the snow instead of sinking."

Anything that had to do with Indians sounded swell to James and he was all for that idea.

It was a whole other world in the woods as the bleakness of the fields in which they had been working gave way to a domain that offered excitement and possibilities around every tree. William showed James how to spot the deer tracks explaining how each print was like an arrowhead pointing in the direction that the animal had gone. He pointed out fresh tracks and ones several days old, tracks of large deer and small, bucks and does.

Pulling the boy over to a sapling, he indicated a deer rub where a buck had worn away the bark with his antlers, and told him that there was always some worn twigs above these rubs where the stag would rub his eye glands leaving his scent like a calling card.

"How big was this guy?"

James was perplexed by the question. He could see no new prints, so was at a loss to even guess.

William put his arm around the boy's shoulders. "When you look at a rub, the bigger the thickness of the tree, the bigger the deer. Also, look at the height of those worn twigs he used for his eyes. Imagine how tall he would have to be to reach up there."

He began circling the trees in the area like a dog looking to relieve himself. "Usually there is a scrape nearby where that same buck will paw at the ground and piss in the spot making sure that he has left his scent as a mark of his territory. It scares the other males away and attracts the does. Have you ever smelled deer piss?" Without waiting for an answer he added, "Phew. It stinks as bad as a skunk."

They continued their walk until, once again, William stopped, reached into the leather pouch and whispered, "Over that knoll, there is a valley with a bunch of cedars. Load up and we'll creep up there. We're downwind so its perfect."

Reaching the top of the hill, James peered down expectantly, his finger poised beside the trigger ready to respond to any movement of brown, but he was disappointed. Nothing. That day he learned that deer hunting is a lot of quiet waiting and watching with very little action. They sat with their backs against two trees gazing at the valley below and, despite the fact that several times James thought he saw movements in the trees, there was nothing; his mind had been inventing the quarry. The first alert seconds, turned into attentive minutes which gave way to daydreaming hours. He found himself shifting regularly to compensate for the numbness which developed in various parts of his body.

His lunch eaten, the hours crept on until the longer shadows began. James was thinking of supper and the warmth of the house and the comfort of a chair when he felt a hand squeezing his arm. Turning he followed the path of the pain to a finger pointing towards the trees and he squinted his eyes, unable to distinguish any difference.

William slowly raised his rifle to his shoulder. It seemed to take forever for him to complete the move. He removed the mitt from his right hand and peered down the length of the barrel. James could see his breath regularly leaving his mouth as he breathed in and out, in and out, in and out, and then he stopped. The excitement of the moment blocked out all other thoughts, feelings or memories until the deafening crack of the rifle disturbed the serenity of the scene.

James was conscious of a crashing and movement in the brush. He began to get up until, once again, the hand on his arm stilled him. "Wait. I think I hit her but we wait. I think it's a doe. If I missed, she may come back to this same spot to feed. If she's bleeding, we'll have an easy trail to follow in the snow; she'll go on a bit and then lie down and die. If we start chasing her, she will keep going on pure will and we'll loose her in the marsh."

James filled the next twenty minutes bombarding William with question after question surrounding the sighting and shooting of the deer until he fairly danced down the hill following William to the spot that he had last seen the doe.

Almost immediately William pointed to a crimson speck, ominously obvious in the white snow, walked a few paces and pointed to another and another and another. As they headed into the cedars, James spied a larger stain like a black puddle in the frozen white.

"Ah, that's a good sign," William enthused, kicking at it with his boot. "A heart or lung shot. She won't have gone far."

Thirty more paces they came upon the fallen doe, large brown eyes, purple lolling tongue drooping out the side of the mouth, smooth gray coat and the one small red imperfection. "God, she's small." It wasn't a display of sympathetic remorse, it was a simple statement, an observation. They had experienced a good day, a successful hunt for this was another crop available to the settlers of the Chignecto Basin and they had harvested it.

After a lesson in cleaning and gutting the animal, William showed him how to insert a stout sapling through the tendons of the back legs. Each shouldering an end of the pole, they triumphantly carried back the carcass to the house, congratulating each other on their hunting prowess. Once there, additional processing provided the sweet, gamy taste of venison and a hide to be cured and utilized.

"Deer aren't the only game that are tasty. Come and I'll show you how we get some rabbits for a pie. That's my favourite."

William showed James how to wax a bit of string with a candle which added stiffness allowing the strand to be formed through a slip knot into a firm loop. These were attached to small stakes and set as snares along the numerous rabbit runs visible in the underbrush, with the hope that a dozen of these set out at night would result in a couple of captured animals in the morning. As well as rabbit stew and pies which William fancied, Sarah sewed the pelts to make white fur muffs for Elizabeth and herself.

These hunting expeditions continued through the winter and the promise of another excursion was the carrot that motivated William and James to abide the tree clearing which dominated their days. Moose, deer, rabbits, squirrels, geese and ducks each had their seasons and provided many pleasant diversions in each other's company. James made the best of his opportunities which caused William to comment to a neighbour, "The boy is quite a shot. There might not be any game left by the time young Rufus can hold a gun."

Remembering the events of 1812, the neighbour replied, "Maybe he will be forced to go after bigger game."

About the middle of March the snow was beginning to recede, finally surrendering to the lengthening and warming days of spring. The day that they had been anticipating finally arrived and the whole household came out to welcome Charles Bulmer as he led the two year old ox up the path to his new home at Fawcett farm.

While Rufus sucked his thumb and clung to his mother, Elizabeth hopped about excitedly. "What's his name? What will we call him?"

William took her hand in his and said, "Oxen are usually named Buck or Bright and I think that we'll name this one Buck, however, I suspect that we best leave that decision to James as the ox is going to be his to train. I have enough to do around here and I think the experience would be good for you, James."

James swelled up with pride. He was enjoying each new trust and responsibility that William gave him. During the next few weeks he spent all his spare time with the ox, grooming him, feeding him and cleaning his stall. The animal learned to tolerate James working around him and with him, and started to trust the young lad. With William's help, he fitted the ox to a light yoke with two chains leading back and, in no time, Buck got used to dragging these around the feed yard as he appeared to be eager to please the boy. As James walked behind he would call "Gee Buck" and the ox would turn right or he would cry "Haw Buck" and the ox would turn left. James was quite patient with the beast and William observed, "I find it hard to discern who is more proud, the ox or James. He does everything for that animal except wipe its nose."

All was going very well until it came time to teach Buck to pull a load. James fastened the chains to a log and tried to get Buck to pull. He led Buck, but as soon as the animal felt the resistance of the log behind, he would stop. No amount of encouragement would cause the ox to pull against the weight. James tried pleading with the animal, tempting him with food, standing behind him and shouting, even pushing him while

Elizabeth tried to lead. Buck would drag the chains happily all day, but not pull a load.

In desperation, James cut a piece of sapling and trimmed all the branches. He stood on the left side holding the reins, yelled "Up Buck" and struck him with the switch. The surprised Buck circled to his right to avoid the stick, tangling himself in the chains and log. Whenever he would see that switch, he would circle away from it, but never pull the log.

"Help him, William," Sarah begged. "He needs some guidance. The two are getting exasperated with each other and I don't want to see James quit in failure."

James was frustrated. He persisted hour after hour but each time it would end in his screaming at Buck and them both stopping in defeat. James was disappointed with the ox and even more annoyed with himself for falling short in the task that William had given him. Yet he continued.

Finally, William joined James as he sat discouraged outside the barn and asked, "James, you're smarter than that damn ox. Why won't he pull?"

James dejectedly kicked at a stone at his feet. "It's not Buck's fault. It's me, I guess I'm just not any good at this."

William persisted. "James, he will do anything for you. I have seen you around the animal. But why do you think he stops when he feels that log behind him. Isn't he strong enough? Can't he do it? Is Buck a weakling? Why do I see other oxen pull loads ten times that weight?"

James flushed in anger as he protected his ox. "He's young and he's plenty strong. He just doesn't know how strong he is."

"Exactly," William exclaimed. "That ox is not so different from you. I never give you a job that you can't do. When you first came to us, we had you do simple chores and then moved you up to more difficult tasks. We let you succeed. The same with Buck. He has to know that he can pull through any job that you give him. Come with me."

William harnessed Buck and backed him to the corner of
the barn where he put one length of the chain on one side of
the corner pole and the other length on the other side and then
connected the two pieces of chain with a small twig.

"Now watch what happens when Buck pulls."

As he led the animal forward, Buck felt a very slight
resistance and then the stick snapped. William praised the
ox.

"See. He felt the load but was successful in pulling away.
We must make him feel that he can always break the stick.
Shortly, he will put his full weight behind doing just that."

James repeated the exercise over and over, very gradually
increasing the size of the stick that held the chains to the post.
Each time Buck pulled just a little harder to make the stick
snap. He loved the game and responded quickly to the success
and the praise and soon he, too, was pulling his weight.

A few days later James approached William and, looking
down at his boots, he said, "I'm sorry that I messed up with
Buck. I'll do better next time."

William smiled and, punching him lightly in the shoulder,
he said, "You didn't mess up, son. You're learning, too.
Mistakes are okay."

James was ecstatic, he was bursting with happiness and
didn't hear anything else that William said. Had it been a
mistake? William had called him "son".

Elizabeth smiled from the doorway of the house and held
her mother's hand. Sarah wiped a tear from her eye. Rufus
pouted and cried.

Chapter XI

As the months and years changed, James learned the new demands of each successive season, the plowing and planting, the birth of animals, feeding and cleaning, weeding and cultivating, the constant repair of tools and machinery, cutting and harvesting. With every new decision and problem, James and William worked together and worried together. Would there be enough rain? Would there be too much rain? Was it the right time to plant? Should they harvest now? Would the insects kill the crops? William often sought and relied on the opinions of his young helper.

It was the summer of 1822 and James was repairing a wagon wheel in the yard when he heard an ominous squeal. "Sarah, the gun. Get the gun." He grabbed a pitchfork and ran to the barn. "William. William. Pigs in the woods. Wolves. Bears. I think they got one." Sarah met the two men in the yard and they headed in the direction of the unearthly shriek which was getting louder every second.

Often the hogs, looking for more or different food, wandered into the woods and had to be rounded up and returned. The big danger was wolves or bears who loved nothing more than a pork meal, fat and tasty, and so easy to catch. Everyone got used to checking the hogs each time they were outside, doing a quick count and more than once they had to go searching. The sound of this squeal was hated and feared.

"God that's loud! Damn them. It must be a big hog." Running now, William loaded his gun while continuing to move through the field. The high pitched sound pierced the air sending shivers up and down their spines as they visualized the ravaged animal bloody and torn apart yet continuing to cry in pain and terror. Sarah sounded the alarm summoning help from neighbours. What would they find? Still the sound persisted, still louder and louder.

Suddenly James and William stopped. They dropped their weapons, looked at each other and collapsed on the ground in gales of laughter. An ox-cart rounded the bend and headed up the path to the farm with its wooden axles so dry that they emitted a high pitched squeal as the result of the wheels turning in protest. One of the many vendors who travelled the province selling their wares was drawing near and this one did not need a bell to announce his arrival; the intensity and sound identical to a dying hog.

These peddlers were a source of information and gossip as they hawked their goods from farm to farm. General stores were still a rarity and the sight of the peddler was always welcome since he carried with him all the hard goods that were required to run a farm and a house.

As the peddler quaffed a second mug of cider which he had liberally laced with his own stock of rum, James applied a thick coating of grease to the axle to prevent some other farmer experiencing the same alarm. The Fawcetts picked over his stock as the man told them of a fire at Magegadavic Settlement in southwestern New Brunswick where the season had been excessively dry so the farmers had set little fires to rid their lands of the stumps in their fields. He told them of how the winds had come up and what had been several small fires became one huge inferno, consuming woods and fences and sending panic to the residents who rallied to try and save their homes. Apparently some sparks carried half a mile to fall upon the wooden shingles of a house where the inhabitants had to escape to safety to wait out the night and the fire.

The peddler, an accomplished storyteller, had their attention now and whether the cider or the truth or the desire to carry through with a good yarn prevailed, he continued his story.

"A young man drunk and travelling alone came to the burning house where, insensible to the danger, he went inside and was overcome by the smoke and flames and he perished. He was found the next morning, as black and charred as a burned root with his clothes scorched off and his shoes still on his feet. Any facial features were beyond recognition and his body was so twisted and disfigured that a special coffin had to be built to accommodate him. His grotesque limbs could not be bent and made to squeeze inside the regular box."

Sarah and Elizabeth listened with white faces and open mouths while James and William shook their heads in disbelief. Meanwhile Rufus had worked loose a box of nails from the peddler's cart which he proceeded to dump all over the ground. Suddenly the man said something which made time stop for James. At first he couldn't believe his ears as he thought it must be some cruel joke and he stood up from retrieving the nails with a look of horror on his face.

Removing his cap and scratching his balding head, the peddler added, "The fella wasn't from these parts. They say he was a drifter and nobody knows his name. He was a young lad. In fact the only thing he had of any value that wasn't harmed by the fire was a fine bone pocket knife with an army crest. It survived the heat and the flames so they gave it to the man who made the coffin."

The family stared at James as he sank to the ground, beads of sweat breaking out on his forehead. He suddenly felt cold and clammy and knew he would be sick as he sat with his head between his legs and the old thoughts and memories, the feelings and uncertainties, flooded back to his consciousness; those dark days that he had done so well in forgetting, in blanking out, rushing back because of one story uttered by a stranger. Would he ever be oblivious to them, able to deal with them? Could he ever forget?

James rose to his feet and stumbled behind the barn where he dropped to his knees and vomited. As he spit the vile liquid from his mouth and coughed to soothe his raw throat, he knew that an unfinished part of his life had been brought to a terrible and horrible conclusion. He wasn't sure if he was glad or whether he felt cheated that he had now lost an opportunity for sweet revenge. He felt badly that he was so vengeful that he could harbour these desires for retribution for so long.

William sat down beside him. James buried his face in his hands and, between sobs, related his fears, his suppositions, the hidden facts of his life gone past. He told William about the drowning, his guilt, the home, the friendship gone awry and he found solace in relating the tale to this man whom he had grown to love. It was as if, in sharing it, he no longer had to bear the burden alone.

"James, you've been with us six years now and you've got to know how we feel about you. You are one of our family." He gripped the young man's arm and continued, "There won't be any peace for you until you rid yourself of all your guilt and fears. You know that I am a religious man and it may not be for you but it is only through becoming involved with the church that I found harmony in my life. There's a man at the meeting house that I think you should talk to."

So, at the age of nineteen, James spoke to James Priestly and was converted to Methodism. Although he had gone to church as did all the members of the community young James had never really internalized the teachings. In a pragmatic way he reasoned that if by joining the church now he felt a little better and if it pleased William, it was probably a wise move. He did feel a certain serenity and calm that he had never had, and William, in particular, thought of and accepted James as his son. William expressed this to his brother, John, after church one Sunday.

"How is young Anne doing? I hear that she and Isaac are keeping you in grandchildren."

"I only wish that they lived a little closer. Young Will might be the next to get married. He has his eye on a young thing from over Cornwallis way. I wouldn't be surprised if they got married. Your hired man, James is about the same age. Has he a special girl? What's he doing?"

"James has no steady girl yet. He's still young though I guess you heard that he joined our church. I can only hope that Rufus will learn from him and become like James. He is everything that a man could want in a son. He is honest and hardworking. Sarah and I are so proud of him."

"But he isn't flesh and blood," John cautioned. "You must be true to your own family first. Don't let him use you. You have given him so much, I wouldn't want to see you betrayed."

"Betrayed?" William repeated. "That boy has brought far more to our family than we could ever hope to repay. The success of the farm is greatly to his credit. There is enough love in our home to embrace James as well."

"But he's not a Fawcett. Rufus is your future."

"Things will work out fine."

"Ever the optimist, William. It always was your strength."

"Ever the critic, Johnnie. Distrust can be a weakness."

"As can mistrust, William," warned John. "Some of our family members need more love and attention than the others and you should think on that. Let us leave it and let no more be said."

The brothers shook hands and joined their respective families, both conscious of the rift that was beginning to develop.

Later when William discussed this exchange with Sarah, she added, "Johnnie has opinions on everything and I wouldn't let it bother me. However it would be a shame if this ever came between you two. You have always been the peacemaker in the family. Having said that, I, too, am concerned about Rufus."

William shuffled his feet nervously and looked up at the worried face of his wife. "He is not an easy child to love, Sarah. There is no peace when he is about, whereas James seems to do the right thing at the right time. I don't think he cares much for Rufus either."

Sarah jerked her head back as she felt her heart skip a beat. "Either." She had heard her husband correctly and this was the first time that William had ever admitted that he didn't like Rufus. "Either." She briefly considered challenging William on this point but decided to consider what he had said and leave it for a calmer time. Sarah was aware of how others regarded Rufus and she had always protected him, believing that his moods and behaviours were phases, times that he would soon outgrow. Now the shock of confronting truths for the first time repeated in her own house by her own family, cast a cloud over her feelings. She was angry and confused as she had something new to brood about.

Now aware of how William regarded Rufus, Sarah found additional occurrences that demonstrated what she had just learned. She analyzed each statement, each behaviour by both her husband and her son to try to gain an insight into their relationship. Unwittingly, she caused the schism to grow by protecting Rufus from having to deal with his father.

When William suggested that they go hunting, Sarah would say, "I really need him to help me here in the house today. You and James go."

When William announced that the three of them were chopping trees or working in the field, Sarah responded, "I need Rufus to take the wagon into town today for some supplies."

Often his studies became a way of protecting him from these interactions. "He really should stay inside and read."

He was the first to attend the new school at Crane's Corners and Sarah would often remark, "Mr. Pendleton says that Rufus has real ability and that, if he would just spend more time at his studies, he could become quite a scholar." It wasn't clear whether the schoolmaster could actually control Rufus or if he was merely trying to protect the forty shillings a year that he received for putting up with the boy. Regardless, it was a convenient technique that permitted Sarah to guard her son from confrontations with William.

So in the subsequent months and years, William and Rufus actually had less to do with each other. Left to everyday living, they might have worked things out early, but each day made that possibility less and less probable. William knew that it was wrong, he knew that he was wrong but, after all, he had James to keep him company and with whom to share his work and his hopes and his dreams.

James was rather naive regarding relationships. He was lost in his days with William and adored Elizabeth while avoiding Rufus at every opportunity. It wasn't that he hated Rufus, he just didn't like the way he treated everyone including his family.

Christmas of 1823 brought another one of the family get togethers. James was twenty and he and young Will had become good friends, partly because they were the same ages and partly because they were similar easy-going personalities.

"Have you and Uncle William tracked down that big buck yet?"

"The Gray Ghost?" James and Will had both adopted a habit of pinning pet names on anything that moved in the province. "We saw the tracks by the knoll but no luck yet. He's a wary old bugger and, besides, I don't want to shoot him before your uncle has a chance." The young men grinned at each other. "When are you coming over for a hunt? I haven't seen you all fall."

Will squirmed a little in his seat and suddenly became serious. "I've been spending time at Annapolis Valley. Alice Chase and I are getting married next month. Eunice and Thomas are standing up for us but I want you to be there. Maybe you would accompany Little El for me." Long ago the boys had begun referring to Will's sister Eleanor as Little El to distinguish her from Elleanor, Will and Eleanor's mother. Although they had once called the elder woman Big Ell, the lack of wisdom of using that nickname was made apparent to them in no uncertain terms.

James flushed slightly for Eleanor was an attractive young girl who had the eye of many of the young men. "Congratulations. It is not totally unexpected. I guess that would be no real hardship to look after Little El. Do you think she would mind?"

"Here you go again, James." Will smiled. "Give yourself a little credit, just keep your hands off her, she's only sixteen."

The next few weeks were not happy ones for James. He seemed more moody than usual, with his nervousness increasing each passing day. He was quiet and the rest of the family noticed the times that he sat alone staring into the fire or pushing his food moodily about his plate and displaying his irritability.

"What's the problem?" Sarah asked one evening after the supper dishes had been cleared. "You have been moping around here lately."

James brushed some dirt from his pant leg. "It's the wedding."

"You'll still see Will," William replied. "He's not dying. He's only getting married."

Flustered, James said softly, "It's not that. It's just that there will be dancing after the wedding and I'm supposed to be looking after Eleanor."

Sarah smiled and, putting her hand on James's sleeve, she said gently, "That's no problem. We can look after that, can't we Elizabeth?" Elizabeth flashed a broad smile and nodded.

Each night, after the meal was over, they pushed back the low table and worked with James. William moved off to another part of the house to read while Rufus provided a commentary of the events. As Sarah and Elizabeth showed James where to put his hands and how to move his feet, he learned all the dance steps. However, as he held Elizabeth and moved about the room, he was shocked to look into her face. He stared at her as if he had never seen her before because, without him noticing, she had begun to mature and become a young lady.

Her face was more angular. The round chubby appearance had developed a more mature softness that he found quite appealing.James tried to remember when she had started to change. Her hair was still the same striking black that was so distinctive, her nose still tipped up at the end, but she was no longer cute, she was beautiful. He looked away confused by these strange thoughts.

"Where did a girl of thirteen learn to dance like this?" he asked while moving his feet awkwardly to prevent stepping on her.

"Oh, they teach us this while you men are out hunting in the woods." She chuckled, pushed herself away and broke the moment, "I think he is ready to stir the hearts of all the girls in New Brunswick."

As James reddened, Rufus put his finger in his open mouth and grunted, "Yech."

On January 20, 1824, William Fawcett married Alice Chase in the Methodist Meeting House. Everyone agreed that the service performed by Reverend Chris Milner was beautiful, the meal served by the ladies of the church was delicious and the speeches and welcomes, though too long, evoked some humour at Will's expense.

However, James could not remember the details of any of these for his mind was fixated on the upcoming dance as he went over the sequence of the various dance steps in his mind. He stole glances at Eleanor every chance that he got.

As he sat nervously on one side of the hall with the other young men, he finally spotted Eleanor sitting on the opposite side with Elizabeth. A bright bow on top of her head, Eleanor's hair hung down in auburn ringlets framing her beautiful, fresh face. James loved the way she tossed her hair out of her eyes in such an alluring fashion. He had never seen her look more beautiful than she did now in her new dress. Her white gloves moved up to shield her mouth as she leaned over to talk to Elizabeth and then, both looked his way and giggled.

A young man began to play the bagpipes and several of Alice's friends from Nova Scotia joined together in some informal jigs, reels and hornpipes. At first James was disturbed by this turn of events, but soon a traditional fiddler and caller replaced the piper and various couples began to get up and dance. He imagined that all eyes were on him waiting for his next move as he tried to bolster his confidence and his nerve. His hands were all sweaty as he wiped them down the legs of his pants. He knew the steps, Elizabeth had spent long enough with him. He could do it; yes, he would do it.

"Don't be an idiot, James." It was Rufus who had slid in beside him. "If you're thinking of asking Eleanor, don't waste your time. I talked to her and Betsy and she doesn't like you. She says no way she would dance with a hired man. She says that labourers like you should dance with servant girls — your own kind."

James's mouth dropped open as he turned to stare at the boy, not wanting to believe what he was hearing. Rufus continued, "She says she wouldn't want to be seen with an orphan boy who has to beg off other people to live."

James looked over to where the two girls were glancing back at him and laughing. His mind whirling, he got up and headed out of the hall not wanting to look anyone in the eye. The walk across the room seemed to be taking forever and he was sure everyone was watching and laughing as he attempted to escape. The air seemed hot and heavy and it was impossible to breathe, if he could only make it to the cold frosty evening outside. He thought he might faint.

Once free of the cruel building, James lowered his head and ran slipping and sliding back to the farm, unconcerned by the snow and the slush. He should have known better and Rufus had brought him back to reality. Why would Eleanor want to dance with him? Why would any young lady want to dance with him? Rufus was right. He was a common labourer, working as a farm hand, who had forgotten his position.

Inside the hall, the girls pulled the young boy down to a chair, while they towered above him. "Where did James go? Why did he leave? Rufus, what did you tell him?"

"I don't know. I didn't say anything. Leave me alone. I just told him what you told me to — that you wanted to dance. I guess he got scared and left."

As Rufus went off to join some friends over at the tables of food, he didn't notice the look of disbelief on the girls' faces, nor did he see the tear running down his sister's cheek.

Chapter XII

Young men customarily married at about twenty-one years of age while young women often married by eighteen. Certainly, many married younger than this age and it was not unusual for girls to marry at fifteen or sixteen, particularly if they wanted to escape the home. Sons, particularly the eldest, often lived on the home farm that they stood to inherit as their birthright.

The lure of the city was present in Sackville as it was elsewhere. Saint John and Halifax were constant sources of adventure and excitement while some of the parts of Canada to the west were only dreams for the most adventuresome.

It was 1828 and four years had passed since Will's wedding. Eleanor was now married. Their mother Elleanor had died but Johnnie was remarried within the year to Emily Terrice who was twenty-one years his junior. James enjoyed his life on the Fawcett farm and, since Rufus had set him straight on his station in life, he harboured no illusion of landing one of the beautiful, proper girls in the Sackville area. He was, for all intents and purposes, running the everyday operation of the farm. William was increasingly involved with the new Sackville and Westmorland Agricultural Society which began to use its buying power to procure seeds and animals. He continued to treat James as a son asking him his opinion on all the matters pertaining to the administration of their joint means of livelihood.

"The Society has negotiated an unbelievable price for timothy, clover, wheat and oat seed. The quantities will be limited this first year so we must submit our order soon."

James rubbed his chin as he looked out over the flock of sheep. "I would like to concentrate on the clover and put those ewes out for breeding. If we were to butcher the male lambs and build up our herd with the females, we would be in good shape for that new ram that they are talking about. Why don't you talk to Trueman and get us first breeding when the Society brings the ram in?"

To Elizabeth, now eighteen, James was her best friend as well as a confidant. "Why don't you get to know Maria Copp? She's a nice girl and I could arrange to introduce you."

"Now I heard that George Reed was sweet on you and he was fixing to ask your father for your hand." Continuing to try to deflect the conversation, James added, "I've got so much work here on the farm, I don't know where I'd fit a wedding, anyway."

"James stop it. I know when you are trying to change the subject. You have to get out more. Father can handle things here, Rufus is fourteen now and it's time he began to get more involved in the farm. This is going to be all his some day."

"And I'll be still here working for him. He'll need somebody to do the dirty work. I don't think he is much into farming. A government job behind a desk is more to his liking."

Sarah continued to be the conciliator in the family. She spent her time trying to mediate the events of everyday living between Rufus and his father however, not much had changed.

William had no time for a lazy, difficult child and Rufus had no desire to work hard in the mud and the dirt of an Atlantic farm. Still Sarah tried. "James, will you watch over Rufus and try to teach him the ways of the farm? I am afraid that William hasn't much patience for the young boy, but Rufus needs to learn."

"I have tried before. You know he doesn't listen to me. I don't really think he's interested."

"Give him half a chance. He looks up to you as an older brother."

Unconvinced, but out of respect for Sarah, James would try again to show Rufus how the farm was run, but the result was predictable.

As James tried to explain the proper time to seed, Rufus asked, "Let me get this straight. This farm will be all mine some day. Right?"

"You know that, Rufus."

"Now this farm is worth a lot of money. Am I right?"

Not liking the direction of this conversation, James replied, "Well, yes. The land is good and your father has a good breeding program going."

"I mean, the land, the animals and everything have a value."

Letting the new seed filter through his fingers, he paused thoughtfully, "I suppose so. What's your point?"

Heading out of the barn with a satisfied smile on his face he concluded, "When my father dies, I'll hire labourers like you or I'll sell it all and head west. I'll be rich."

Family life on the Fawcett farm continued with scarcely enough time to accomplish the daily and seasonal chores without William and James being overly concerned about feelings and relationships. They were content to continue, to maintain the status quo, and not change, however, life is never static and time does not stand still.

It was September of 1830, when Sarah announced that Elizabeth was bringing home a special guest for Sunday dinner. William and James were too involved with the harvest season to devote much time or thought to this and they both regarded it as an imposition that they would need to dress in their best for the evening meal. Though they didn't work on Sunday, James had learned from William and used the day to get ready for the upcoming week by planning, readying tools and carrying out minor repairs and preparations.

"Harding Bishop is coming to dine with us and Rufus, I want you home for dinner." Sarah busied herself polishing the silverware that she had inherited from her mother. "William, please try to stay inside after the meal and no excuses about something needing tending in the barn. James, he is a special friend of Elizabeth's, so no teasing."

Even the dogs sensed that there was something special about this particular meal and disappeared to the woods to chase some rabbits where there would be no one to yell at them or tell them to move. William and James took a walk to the front field to see how the second cut of hay was drying. The familiar landscape was considering dissolving to pleasant autumn tones of red, brown and yellow.

"Young Elizabeth is growing up. Did you see her in that new dress today? I am afraid that no man is safe once she and her mother get to fussing." William stopped to feel some of the bunches stooked near the fence. "It won't be long until it's just the men left for Sarah to mother. Now that's a thought."

Before this moment it had never occurred to James that Elizabeth would someday leave Fawcett farm. He paused and looked out across the marsh which was beginning to evidence the death of summer. "Sometimes I wish that things wouldn't change. There has been so much diversity in my life that I sometimes covet some boring repetition. I guess I never really thought that Betsy would want to leave the farm."

"It's not a case of want, son. This Bishop lad is from Albert County and is a schoolmaster so, if she were to marry him, she, like every other new bride, would go to live with her husband or husband's family." As an afterthought he added, "Eligible young men are few and far between in this area."

"It's just that things will be different around here. I've gotten kind of used to her. She's a good friend."

William ran his fingers down the stalk of hay sending small seeds flying up in a spray. "Maybe too much a friend, more like a sister? You best face facts that, like the weather, times are going to change and just as fiercely, but without as much warning. I am sixty now so you, yourself, must look ahead. Twenty-seven is ancient for a single man."

James chuckled. "You're getting to sound like Elizabeth now. Enough of this marrying talk. Let's go back to the house and prepare to meet this young man."

James had certain preconceived notions of how a school teacher was supposed to look and behave but the man whom he met in the parlour of the Fawcett farm destroyed these assumptions in seconds. Harding Bishop was tall with brown hair that was slicked down and combed in the fashion of the day. James ran his hand carelessly through his own unruly mop that refused to stay where it was put. Harding had the refined good looks that one did not find in the faces of the local farmers who spent their days in the extremes of temperature and weather. His suitcoat hung on his broad shoulders in a way that showed off the material to its best advantage while not disguising the muscular stature of the man who wore it. His pants had a crease that could only be achieved if the man had carried his trousers and dressed at the gate rather than the reality of having worn them and sat in them for hours on horseback over the dusty paths and roads. And his boots — the black leather gleamed and glistened in stark contrast to James's own which had long ago given up any attempt to demonstrate their original colour.

As James strode forward to shake his hand, the man's slender fingers gripped his callused hand in a firm grasp that was accompanied by a friendly and disarming smile. The movement caused his suitcoat to part, revealing a gold watch chain emerging from his waistcoat. "I am very pleased to meet you Mr. George. Elizabeth speaks very kindly of you and credits your shrewd farming methods in a large part for the success of this homestead."

His voice was like velvet and there was an ingenuous quality to his words which immediately subdued and seduced the listener while his eyes were bright and clear as they transferred all attention to the other young man. It was going to be hard to hate him. James looked up trying to be equally engaging, "Please call me James, my father was Mr. George." His weak attempt at humour failed miserably. "Well I think that your career as a schoolmaster is much more important and rewarding than the hard, dirty, menial work that we do in the fields."

Harding flashed a smile that made James feel at ease. If there was any guile in Harding Bishop he was doing a masterful job of disguising it. "I suspect that you are being rather modest, James. I was brought up on a farm in Horton, Nova Scotia, and I could not help but notice your use of peat and mussel mud for fertilizer in that front field of oats. That ought to improve your yield by twenty to thirty per cent in the first year. They were just starting to admit the value of fertilizer at home so you are well advanced."

James flushed with pride. It was going to be hard to dislike this man. Elizabeth smiled demurely.

Turning to William, Harding continued, "Sir, I hear that your establishment of an Agricultural Society plus your actions on behalf of the preservation of the salt marshes have advanced agronomy in the Sackville region."

William beamed. It was going to be hard not to like this man.

The visitor even handled Rufus well. His smooth and charming manner deflected the boy's sarcasm and Harding listened to the lad's opinions with a genuine interest.

At the dinner table he knew, instantly, the right thing to say and the right thing to do. "Mrs. Fawcett, I am surprised that you aren't all as fat as your hogs with your wonderful cooking. I thought that the recipe for Yorkshire pudding as light and fluffy as this had been left in Britain." The ladies appeared to hang on his every word.

Even James's occasional attempts to reveal the flaws in his character had the opposite effect. "Harding, how is it a man like you has avoided marriage?"

"Well, James, I guess my studies in Massachusetts have interfered with my having much of a social life. And, more importantly, until this very moment I have not met a lady who intrigued me as much as our Elizabeth." Elizabeth blushed with pleasure.

After the meal, Harding and Elizabeth went outside in the cool September evening to sit and watch the stars. James found a reason to check the barn and stood in the shadows of the structure where he could see the front porch. He envied Harding his handsome features and genteel ways and, when Harding bent down and gently kissed Elizabeth, James was angry and confused. He genuinely liked Harding, however he was perturbed with Elizabeth.

Almost every weekend, they saw Harding Bishop. When he was not visiting Elizabeth, she found some excuse to go down to visit friends over his way. John Fawcett had become quite fond of the young man as well, providing accommodation for him on his visits. He seemed quite enthusiastic about Harding and tried his best to encourage his niece to further the relationship. "You are indeed fortunate, Elizabeth. He is so very well thought of and would be a welcome addition to our family. I know that your grandfather

Fawcett would approve of your choice and would give you his blessing if he were alive."

"Now, Uncle, let's not move this along too fast. Nothing has been decided yet. He hasn't even asked me."

"I know. Emily and I have enjoyed his visits and I think that I have come to know Mr. Harding Bishop. I would not be surprised to hear that he had popped the question come spring."

"However, it's a long winter, Uncle."

James found that his chats with Elizabeth were less frequent now. He had deliberately avoided her since she had met her new beau despite the fact that James, too, anticipated Harding's visits and thoroughly enjoyed the conversations and activities that the two young men shared. Whether it was hunting, fishing, farming or any other topic, the young teacher was an expert yet he was so charming and genuine that everyone liked him. Since she had been seeing Harding, James felt that she no longer needed him to fulfill the role of friend and comrade.

Finally Elizabeth pushed the issue. She sat across from James after William had attended to their evening devotions and demanded, "What is it James? We never talk any more. I enjoyed our chats together. Did I do something to offend you?"

James squirmed uncomfortably in his chair. "No. I don't know. It's just that, I guess I didn't think that it was appropriate for me to be talking with you all the time, what with Harding and everything."

"Don't be silly. We aren't married yet though it seems as if everyone is trying to push towards that end. Don't you like Harding?"

"Like? The man is amazing. How could anyone not like him? He's perfect. He dresses right, talks right, behaves right. It's like not liking...." He paused looking for the right word.

"Ice cream?" She looked at James for a long time studying the face across from her.

"Yes. That's it, ice cream. Not liking Harding Bishop is like not liking ice cream."

Elizabeth's eyes clouded and she, too, appeared to be trying to find just the right words. She looked down at the Bible in her lap and holding it to her heart, she said softly, "I don't know if I really love him. He's great and all but how do you know? I think my real love is contained in this book."

He nodded in agreement. As Elizabeth put the Bible on the table and left to go to her room, James recalled how she had been accepted into Methodism under the ministry of Sampson Busby and although she had not taken the step lightly, he was rather surprised by what she had just said, by her passionate affirmation of her love for God. He had never heard her speak quite so openly about her religious convictions and had thought that her beliefs, like his own, were more subtle.

Sarah came over from the kitchen area and sat down in front of the fire, interrupting his thoughts. Gazing into the fire, James commented, "I have never heard Betsy talk in so open terms about her love for God."

"You stupid man! Why are you men so stupid, so insensitive?" James looked up, a shocked expression on his face. He would have been no more surprised if Sarah had thrown a bowl of ice cold water over his face. He started to stand, a protest forming on his lips. He opened his mouth but nothing came out.

"You just sit down there and listen to me." Sarah was warming to her topic and James would not have dreamed of disobeying her or interrupting her tirade. He had never seen her behave like this. "I listened to the two of you talking over here. I have watched the two of you dancing around each other, parrying and evading, like two incompetent duelists, each afraid to make the first thrust. Well I'm sick and tired of it and it's going to stop, now. Do you understand?"

James, bewildered, had no idea what she was saying. Sarah, still standing, grabbed Elizabeth's Bible and waved it furiously in front of his face. "Open your eyes. Here is what Betsy meant by her real love being contained in this book."

As she flipped through the pages a soiled packet secured by a small pink ribbon, fluttered to the floor. "Ice cream is something that we all crave once in awhile for dessert, but nobody wants a steady diet of it. Meat and potatoes, those are the staples that we live on. That's the main fare." With that Sarah stormed out of the room.

James still sat. Not sure of what he had heard, not sure of what he had seen. His mouth slowly opening and closing, opening and closing, like a fish out of its environment, gulping for air. He turned to William for support who, instead, rose and turned to follow Sarah. He stopped and paused long enough to say, "I guess that cleared the air some."

Chapter XIII

After the shock and realization of the truth, the relationship between James and Elizabeth began to flourish. Harding Bishop was forgotten as the winter weather cooperated by creating a natural barrier to prevent his visits. Elizabeth spent as much of her day as possible working with James out on the farm as well as assisting her mother in the house, but the two lived for the evenings, when they would sit by the fire or at the table and talk, lost in the presence of each other.

"When did you know?" he asked holding her hand.

She smiled. "Would you believe me if I told you that it was when you returned King?"

"You were only six and I was thirteen." James grinned. "I thought maybe it was when you saw the skillful way that I handled Mr. Harding Bishop when I first met him, and reduced him to a blabbering idiot."

"Well, that was something to behold. How about you? When did you know?"

"For sure?"

"Yes, for sure."

James laughed, "I guess when your mother hit me across the head with the plank to get my attention." He became suddenly serious. "I still must talk to your father. I want to marry you, Betsy, more than anything in this world, but I also want to care for you, provide for you and build you a home. I don't know what he will say."

"Don't worry about it. Things will work out. I am sure that we can borrow enough money from him to buy a piece of land and get started. As long as we are together, I'm not troubled."

Amazingly, Rufus seemed to be completely in favour of the union and encouraged them. "James, I think it's great. You and Betsy can move out and start your own place. I am sure that father and I can run things here. There are plenty of men around looking for manual work. Mother will talk him into lending you the money and you can pay us back next year or even the year after. A lot of people are talking about Upper Canada, have you thought of moving west and settling there?"

When James decided to talk to William and Sarah he was still skeptical but, with Elizabeth's encouragement, he finally built up his nerve. As they stood at the worn pine table, James fumbled for the words to begin. "Betsy and I have been talking..., that is, with your permission..., I would like..., er, we would like to talk to you about our getting married. Now I know that I don't have a...."

Mercifully, James never had to try to finish his speech as William and Sarah rescued the conversation.

"Of course you have our permission."

"We think it's wonderful."

"We thought you were never going to get this thing settled."

"How about spring of '31 for the wedding?"

"We are so happy. It is exactly what we wanted."

Finally William got them all seated and continued, "Now I know that you are concerned about where to live and so on. Sarah and I have been talking about this and we feel that for the first while you should live here and worry about things later. These things have a way of working themselves out, so let's not be too concerned about the details. Get married and then we'll see what happens. Rufus isn't ready to take over the farm yet, anyway, and I need your help."

And so it was settled. With the date of the marriage set as May 21, 1831, the preparations started. The planning was easy as there was no groom's family to please so Sarah and Elizabeth worked out the wedding details while William and James worked on the farm. All was peaceful at the Fawcett farm because they were all busy and no one had time to be overly concerned about Rufus which suited him just fine. He didn't mind a bit, he spent his days planning the takeover of the farm and the spending of the wealth.

Not everyone was pleased with the announcement of the upcoming marriage, as William discovered when he spoke to John one evening after Sunday dinner. "Johnnie, I see that William has presented you with a third grandson. That is some luck. And Alice is well?"

"Emily and I are so happy that they are living with us. Elleanor would have been very proud of them. But that reminds me, I haven't seen young Bishop around lately."

"That is now in the past. We have an announcement; Elizabeth and James are getting married."

John, visibly shocked, pulled William aside. "Married? Are you serious? Why he is an orphan, a worker, a boy from the home. William, I said nothing when you and Sarah took this waif in and treated him as one of the family, but married? He isn't of sufficient means to marry a Fawcett." The words tumbled out as Johnnie tried every means to convince his younger brother of the folly of this union. "How far is Christian charity supposed to extend? What you have done for the boy is admirable, more than any one person would be expected to do and I would be the first to congratulate you but, to give him your only daughter, too. What is his future? What can he be expected to make of himself? What would father have said? The boy is a labourer, not one of us."

"Johnnie, I think you have said enough. It is decided and they have my blessing. They have our blessing." William remained calm as he knew that logic was the only successful method of persuading his brother. "They love each other, be happy for them, they certainly are."

"Happy? Love?" John responded incredulously. "What kind of romantic notion is that? Do you think I married Emily out of love once Elleanor died? Marriage is an arrangement, marriage is survival and this land is tough. Elizabeth deserves better for this boy isn't smart enough to raise and support a family and make something of himself."

"Careful." William raised a hand. "You are my brother and I love you, but sometimes you push too much. I respect your opinions, but they are just that — opinions. Do you always have to be right?"

"William, what of young Rufus?" John continued. "You continue to alienate him. He is a Fawcett and deserves your love yet he suffers from lack of your favour. What is to become of him? You will turn him against you. Do not forever be duped by this beggar, this soldier of fortune."

"Enough, Johnnie. Once more we will agree to disagree. However this must be between us and not seep into the love and fellowship of our families." With that he turned and joined the rest inside. Only Sarah recognized the cloud that hung over him and knew that, once again, he was a victim of his elder brother's criticism.

Weddings were important social events in the community and this one was no exception. For weeks ahead, the number of women from the Sackville area that came and went from

Fawcett farm increased as the day drew nigh. First they arrived with bundles and packages containing blankets, linens, clothes, lace, knitting, needle point, every conceivable craft and every possible carved and constructed utensil, container or piece of furniture. Then it was food. Hams, sausages, smoked meat, roasts, chickens, jams, jellies, preserves, baked goods, breads, baskets of vegetables and fruit were brought to the door, each accompanied by a neighbour who shouldn't, but did, stay for coffee or tea and some of Sarah's cookies.

William kept James safely away from the visitors and the commotion, saying that he didn't want to give him any excuse to back out now. Besides, there was plenty of work to do on the farm that did not stop for births or deaths or weddings or celebrations of any kind.

Will arrived the night before the ceremony to take James to the tavern for a drink and, although William declined, Rufus eagerly accepted the invitation. James was surprised that Will had brought his wagon over for the outing as they had done this sort of thing before, but always on horseback. Regardless, they all tumbled on board to leave for the public house. Elizabeth came out and gave her fiancé a kiss, which prompted from Will, "Just like you were going off to war."

Although James was not a frequenter of any particular public house, he had occasionally been to this tavern kept by Mrs. Richardson and Mrs. Humphrey near the Lower Fairfield Road. Upon entering the dim, smoky atmosphere, he was particularly surprised at the familiarity with which Rufus was greeted and the apparent ease with which he dealt with the bar maid.

"Mr. Fawcett, what'll it be?"

"Rye for these two gents and I'll have my usual, Jane."

This brought two glasses of whiskey and one of brandy for Rufus. So that was it. James now realized where Rufus had been spending his evenings and wondered if William knew. Probably not. He hated to think of what he would do or say if he did.

Barely starting to sip their drinks, other young men began to arrive which in itself was not remarkable except that they were all from this area and they were all James's friends, men who lived on the neighbouring farms or who went to the same church. Not bothered by the coincidence of this, he enjoyed the companionship and conversation of Will and Rufus although they seemed to be preoccupied with other matters.

Had he known what was about to happen, it is doubtful if it would have saved him anyway. The men grabbed James, purchased a bottle or two from the tavern owner, paid their bill and dragged their captive out to the waiting wagon. The other patrons stood back grinning, not offering any assistance, not even Sheriff Chandler who shook his head, shrugged and toasted James during the abduction. As a blindfold was put over James's eyes, they pitched him into the back of the wagon where two of the stoutest of the lads sat on him.

"Any last words, James?"

"We trusted you and you go and decide to get married."

"At your age we thought you knew better."

"Be gentle with him boys, we don't want him all bruised up for Betsy."

The wild ride took about half an hour but covered less than two miles. Every five minutes they would stop, raise his head and pour a generous portion of liquor down his throat causing him to swallow and gag; then they would carry on with the journey. Finally, with the same amount of care as they took loading him, they stripped him of his trousers and boots and rolled him off the back of the wagon.

Amidst the hoots and hollers and noise of the departing wagon, he heard, "See you at the wedding tomorrow," and, "Have a good sleep," and, "We'll take good care of Betsy for you."

Finding one's bearings wasn't really that difficult as there weren't many roads and paths around Sackville that James didn't know. When they had stopped, he had seen the direction from which they had come and, furthermore, if you walked far enough you'd eventually come to the bay or a tavern. James wasn't a drinker so he was feeling very happy and not at all concerned with his plight as he stumbled and staggered his way home, whistling and singing.

The next morning James found his pants and boots beside his bed. Nothing was said at the breakfast table until, unable to contain himself any longer, Rufus asked, "How was your evening at the tavern last night? Somehow we got separated." This brought gales of laughter from all the members of the family. Even Sarah was grinning.

James noticed those same smiles on his friends as the gathered for the wedding. Actually, that was about all that he did remember of the ceremony which Chris Milner performed, except that Elizabeth was beautiful. As he gazed into her eyes, her raven hair framing her beautiful face, he felt that he must be the luckiest man in the whole of New Brunswick. That she could, that she would, love him amazed James and, in that moment, he knew that all the troubles and all the hardships that had led up to this event were a small enough price to pay for the happiness that he was now feeling.

The evening careened on with food and drink and dancing. Each guest made a point of coming and talking to James and Elizabeth but most of the niceties were lost amidst the confusion and the celebration of the night. However, a few imprinted themselves into James's mind.

William pulled James aside and with a warm glow both in his eyes and on his face said, "I could not be happier. I feel as if a son and a daughter were wed today. I know that you love Elizabeth and will care for her in a manner that will guarantee and ensure her happiness. May you have a long and bountiful life together."

Sarah looked lovingly from one newlywed to the other and remarked, "I love you both. I will not welcome James to the family as he is already a part of the Fawcett household and should know that. We are staying at John and Emily's tonight so you will have the house to yourself on your wedding night." Her eyes glistened in the lamp light.

Rufus swaggered up to them, obviously enjoying the refreshment. "Betsy, I hope that you and James find a place as fine as this to call your home. I suspect that you will be anxious to get started and anything that I can do, please let me know." Rufus continued, smiling at James, "I am not losing a sister, I am gaining some room." Not one to let things rest, he nudged James. "The farmer's daughter — you have done pretty well for yourself."

Will and Alice smiled at the new couple. "You know that I knew nothing of those horrible happenings last night. I tried to stop them. James, if you need any advice, be sure to ask me as I have a proven breeding record with three fine sons."

Alice blushed and added, "We are very pleased that you are part of the family, James." Turning to Elizabeth she carried on, "I think you made a fine choice, Betsy. We love him."

John was consistent in his outspoken opinions when he said, "Elizabeth, I hope you are happy. If you ever need anything, feel free to come to me. We Fawcetts stick together." To James he commented, "You have married well. Don't discredit William's trust."

It was nearly eleven o'clock by the time that the last guests left. William and Sarah and Rufus said good night and left with John and Emily. Elizabeth put the last of the dishes away and turned to James and said, "I think the time has come for us to go to bed as well."

For quite awhile James had been anticipating and fearing this moment for in all of his twenty-eight years, he had never gone sparking, never had a woman or even had a steady girl friend. Certainly he had thought about it, dreamed about it and had planned in his mind what he would do and what he would say when the opportunity finally presented itself. Now he was not quite sure. His courage had been brighter in the dark of his bedroom.

As he approached their bed, all his designs and intentions disappeared for standing there, in her lacy nightgown, Elizabeth looked so small, so vulnerable, so ravishing. The half light of the single lantern cast a silky glow which seemed to intensify each curve of her face and each bend of her body. He felt his heartbeat quickening as it seemed he was seeing her, feeling her for the very first time. Taking her fine hands in his, James was conscious of the stirring inside as she pressed her body into his, combining their warmth. Elizabeth buried her face in his shoulder and James breathed in the odour of her hair, her smell, her essence. His body quivered and he was afraid.

"Relax, dear. I am so happy to be Mrs. James George. Do you know I used to say that to myself and write your name? Now, it sounds strange."

"I have never been so happy. I still can't believe that I am so lucky. I love you so much."

Elizabeth responded by wrapping her arms around him and holding him tightly. "I love you, too. This day has been wonderful. Whatever life brings, I am sure that we can face it, as long as we're together."

James reached over and extinguished the flame. Leading Elizabeth by the hand, he pulled back the wedding quilt made by the ladies of the church and sat on the edge of the bed. She stepped forward and stood in front of him. As his hands went up to her shoulders he could feel his fingers trembling and shaking as he slipped the top of her nightgown over her shoulders, over her arms and then her breasts. God she was beautiful. His heart was racing and he could feel the pounding as Elizabeth freed her arms and pulled his face to hers so their lips were touching. He could feel her hot breath and taste the sweet moisture of her mouth.

What happened next took several seconds to register on the newlyweds as for them time was at a standstill and they were the only beings that mattered, that existed in the whole universe. However, at that very moment, the stillness and magic of the night, their first night, was interrupted by an unearthly cacophony unlike any noise or sound they had ever heard. Neither could ignore the din. Neither could identify the sounds as time was shattered.

Cowbells shaken on saplings, frying pans beat with sticks, skillet lids clashed as cymbals, small barrels hit with corn husks, whistles, horns, trumpets, drums, shrieks, screams, war cries, yells combined in a harshness of discord. Any item in the town of Sackville that could be used to disturb the quiet of that spring night was being utilized directly outside their window. Friends, neighbours, church members, guests at the wedding, acquaintances who hadn't been invited to the marriage, young and old were producing a startling symphony timed for just the moment when they saw the last lantern extinguished.

"Oh God, a shivaree," exclaimed Elizabeth.

"And their timing is exact," responded James.

The shivaree was rapidly becoming the usual accompaniment to weddings in the area. Originally they had been reserved for couples with a large disparity in their ages or for second marriages or as a way to display displeasure at not being invited to the festivities. Now, they were often riotous affairs with one thing for certain, the couple would be unable to ignore the revelers.

With embarrassed snickers, James and Betsy slipped back into their clothes and lit the candles and lanterns. They opened the doors, brought out the food and drink, and watched as the fiddlers tuned up and the party resumed. Laughing, Will threw his arm over James's shoulders and said, "I tried to stop them."

As the merriment continued into the wee hours of the next day, Elizabeth noticed the look of chagrin on James's face. She leaned into him and, squeezing his hand, she whispered, "As soon as they're gone, I'll make it up to you."

And she did.

Chapter XIV

The summer and fall of 1831 were a blur to James and Elizabeth as the rigors and demands of the New Brunswick farm required that any adjustments to the normal routines happen quickly, or not at all. As a result, daily life at the Fawcett farm proceeded much as it had before the marriage with William and James looking after the farm, increasing their arable land while striving to improve the breeding stock and crop yield, and Sarah and Elizabeth caring for the household, cooking and baking and sewing and knitting. Rufus spent his days avoiding the other four by being a regular at the tavern and courting the eligible and ineligible girls of Sackville. No one at home really minded what Rufus was doing as everyone was happier when he wasn't nearby and, for his part, he wasn't about to tell his family how he was actually spending his days and nights.

At seventeen, Rufus was a good-looking young man. Although he had a pleasant enough face, he still had the body of a boy for he was thin and hadn't developed the muscle definition of the other boys his age, partly because he was slower maturing and partly because he avoided the manual labour of the farm. His friends were acquaintances whom he met at the taverns and, other than them, he kept to himself. He had the reputation of being moody and irritable.

"Your father has been wondering where you have been lately. He says he could use your help in the fields." Sarah had adopted this style of ascribing her own questions and feelings to her husband in the hope of fostering and nurturing the relationship between the two. Recently, a conversation with either one, concerning the other, brought silence from William and hostility from Rufus.

On his part, Rufus was quite happy with this method of interaction. He could play the same game. "Didn't he mention to you that I was looking for a job in town? I have been talking to some people about importing some goods from the States and I think they are going to make a position for me." He knew that his mother wouldn't verify this story with his father and, anyhow, he would always add a little diversion to keep Sarah busy for awhile. "James said something about wanting to leave and set up a tavern and I thought maybe I would go into business with Betsy and him." As outrageous as this tale was, it would cause Sarah to forget her original quest while she charged about trying to test the veracity of his latest fiction.

Married life was agreeing with Elizabeth and gave her added confidence to speak to her mother about these confrontations. "You know that he just makes up these lies to get you going." Wiping her floury hands on her apron she continued, "I sometimes think that the quicker he leaves the farm, the better for all."

"Elizabeth Fawcett. How can you talk about your brother like this, your own flesh and blood? It's hard for him. He's young." Her kneading seemed to take on an added animation as she slammed and pounded the dough. "He sees James and knows that as far as the farm is concerned, he doesn't measure up in your father's eyes so he tries to find an area where he can excel. We all need to know that we can succeed at something."

"I know mother, we've been through this all before. James knows. But we have to face the truth." She sat down. She found herself needing to take added rests lately. "It is causing us worries, too. James and I must think about establishing our own life but what will you do? What will father do? Whenever James broaches the topic, father changes the subject. My brother has no interest whatsoever in being a farmer and has no intention of becoming one."

James did try to talk to William about this, but because of his feeling that he was treading on family business and because of his father-in-law's reluctance to discuss their leaving, he never got anywhere. "You know the more land we clear, the more work we make for ourselves. You would think we'd learn."

"We've done well, James. I hesitate to speculate where this farm would be without you."

"You know, Pa, we really need to talk about this." Pa had become the agreed form of address designed to bridge the awkwardness of names, spawned by the marriage. "Betsy and I must get ourselves established. We have to start to think about a place of our own."

"See those geese, James? They're forming up and heading south already. Winter will soon be upon us and there is no sense of you doing anything until the spring and, if what Sarah tells me is true, there will be a new dimension to our situation by then." The significance of this last revelation was lost on James until a few days later.

Although life had been very good to James lately, he still harboured some of the same insecurities which caused him to doubt himself. He often found that he was blaming himself for others actions. One evening in October, as he and Elizabeth lay in bed still enjoying the newness of exploring each other's body, James murmured softly, "You seem to be on edge lately. Have I done something to offend you. I certainly...."

She placed her hand across his mouth and then moved it aside letting her tongue brush lightly over his lips. She squirmed down lower in the bed and, tossing back the quilt, she sat astride his hips running her fingertips tenderly through the hair on his chest. Allowing her hands to work up his shoulders and run down the strength of his arms, Elizabeth put her fingers on top of his and moved his hands up to cup her breasts. Conscious of his deeper breathing and her own moist reactions she shivered while her hands pulled James's palms down to rest on her stomach. She rested and pressed his hands against her belly. Lowering her lips so that their mouths were almost touching, Elizabeth breathed in hushed tones, "You're going to be a father."

"What?" The word crashed the silence of the night and caused the dog by the hearth to respond with a sharp bark. "I'm, you're going to, we're going to have a baby?" James struggled to sit up almost tossing Betsy to the floor.

"Shhhh," she giggled playfully, "And Will said you didn't know how."

"When? I mean, are you sure? Wow, this is great, Betsy. I never dreamed...."

Rolling off him to lay in the crook of his arm, she said "You didn't think all that practicing was going to make perfect?"

Long after James could hear the quiet sounds of Elizabeth sleeping, he lay beside her, his eyes wide open. How could he possibly sleep with the energy of this news exciting him? More than once he reached over and lightly ran his hand over his wife's stomach. He was going to be a father.

If the rest of the world didn't know James and Elizabeth's news, they might have guessed by the extra tenderness and care with which he treated her, or the expanded vigour with which he attacked his work, or, perhaps, the cheeriness with which he greeted each new day no matter what the weather. There seemed to be a new spring to his step and a tune which he was forever whistling or humming.

Finally, in the first week in January Elizabeth announced, "Mother and I are going over to Uncle Johnnie's for awhile. Alice will be delivering soon and we thought we might stay with her and see if we can help. With three boys, they are really hoping for a girl."

"Is it safe? Are you well enough to travel?" James grasped her hand as he looked into her eyes with concern.

"I am pregnant, not sick. Our baby is three months off. I'm strong and feeling fine. James, don't worry so, I might learn something by being around the children and helping at the birth. Besides, if I don't get away from your constant cheer and ever-present help, I think I will go out of my mind."

So it was settled and Sarah and Elizabeth set off by sleigh to John Fawcett's farm. It was the first time that James and Elizabeth had been apart since the wedding and at first James found it difficult falling asleep without his wife beside him in the large bed. William and James used this opportunity for some more frequent hunting. They both agreed that the meal times were generally not a success as they hastily grabbed something to eat before collapsing in their respective chairs each evening. With William's help, James began building a small cradle with rockers and slat sides in preparation for the birth of their own child. If there ever was, this was a labour of love as he planed down the maple sides to a buttery smoothness.

He was working in the shop attached to the barn during the afternoon of January 15, when he faintly heard the unmistakable jingle of sleigh bells getting ever louder as they approached. As with many common sounds, a farmer could identify by the tone and timbre certain sleighs without even looking. James knew immediately that these bells belonged to the Fawcett horse and ran outside to see the sleigh turn up the lane followed by a powdery cloud of snow. It seemed to take forever to cover the last hundred yards and James could see Sarah and Elizabeth bundled together. Whether it was the speed that they were travelling or their position in the sleigh, James had a premonition of bad news before they came to a halt by the barn.

"Oh, James." Elizabeth was sobbing as she moved into his arms and folded hers around his neck. She continued to cry into the chest of his coat while he held her tightly. His first fears were quickly allayed. He could feel the reassuring roundness of her tummy pushing up against him. Soothing her and gently stroking her hair, he knew better than to speed the story from her before she was ready.

William put his arm around Sarah as they walked slowly to the house talking in hushed tones. James thought that he could count the times on one hand that he had seen the elder Fawcetts hugging each other. Leading Elizabeth by the hand, they sat on the snowy bench outside the barn. He could see her breath rising in rapid puffs of white slowly changing to less frequent larger clouds. She was beginning to compose herself.

"Alice went into labour in the middle of last night. Since it was her fourth and the other three births easy, the doctor wasn't called. They had a midwife but the delivery was a difficult one." Elizabeth sobbed. "There was blood everywhere. Alice become weaker and weaker. The last thing she did was hold her baby daughter. They named it Ellen."

"Oh, God," whispered James. "I'm sorry you had to be there. How's Will?"

"Will was frantic, his wife dead and him with four children, all under the age of seven years. I don't know how he's going to handle it. He went out and got drunk. You could see the tear stains on his face. Oh, James. What can we do?"

"I don't know. I do know Will and he'll want some space right now, some time to come to grips with this and figure things out. He'll want to organize his thoughts and feelings. Will is strong. At least John and Emily are there to help."

The next few weeks were quiet and introspective at the farm. William and James found some complicated problem in which to immerse themselves for hours at a time. Sarah and Elizabeth chose this time to clean and reorganize the kitchen, although finding a dirty, cluttered area to scrub was almost an impossibility. Rufus invoked the usual answer that he was now applying to all problems, he stayed away for days at a time.

As was often the case, the resolution of the predicament was left to Sarah who finally said, "I know that this is a difficult time for us all. We loved Alice and she and Will were a fine couple, but there are four small children in that house who are going to need our help, not our pity. James, Will is counting on you. You are his best friend. A day's hunting wouldn't be misspent."

They each squirmed uncomfortably as she continued, "Elizabeth and I will go over to Johnnie's as frequently as we can to do whatever we can. William, perhaps you should speak to your brother and see if we can help financially although I suspect they are better off than we are in that regard."

Turning her attention to Elizabeth, she concluded, "The unspoken fear is how all this relates to Betsy and her upcoming birth. It doesn't. These things happen and there is no sense or predicting why or when. Betsy, you are strong and there is no reason to believe the worst because of what happened to Alice, so let's all stop dwelling on this and return this house to normal. We have a little over two months to prepare for this new life in our own home so let's concentrate on that and cherish this event even more specially."

With that, they put the incident to rest and life continued on the farm in Sackville. Will's misfortune had affected them, but life and death were common events and it didn't do to cling to either with too much vehemence. Alice Chase Fawcett, thirty-one years of age, was buried in the Four Corners cemetery with the simple inscription "Lord Jesus receive my spirit".

In early April of this same year, 1832, James and Elizabeth marveled at the birth of their first child, a son whom they named William Frederick. Everything went well and, as often is the case, this new arrival changed life as they all knew it.

With Sarah's help and experience, Elizabeth adapted quickly to being a mother. The never ending duties of feeding, washing, cleaning, playing, soothing and comforting dominated her waking hours and it was often the few stolen minutes before falling asleep that James and she coveted.

"I don't know what we would do without your mother. We are so fortunate. I feel useless around wee Willie." They had all agreed on the diminutive "Willie" as a means of distinguishing him from the other Williams.

"Your time will come soon enough." Elizabeth smiled, "I think you and father are already planning his first hunting trip."

"I love you, Betsy, and I love our new son."

"Uh huh," was the last sounds that James heard before they both drifted into an exhausted sleep trying to grab a couple of hours rest before the baby would demand his mother's attention once again.

If mother and father and grandmother fussed with this new life in their home, it was William who doted on his grandson and he did so without embarrassment. During the day he would find excuses to drift to the house for a peek at the sleeping boy. At dusk, he would hustle to the parlour and offer to hold or rock the baby so Elizabeth could help her mother. He was the first to notice that Willie needed changing and did so himself, eagerly. At the first sign of fussing, William would lift him up and tickle and play with him until all was well.

William didn't seem to be able to get enough of this new baby. He loved his softness as he caressed his pink skin delicately with his hardened fingers. He treasured his smell, unlike any other on the farm and yet reminding him of the varied scents of spring so prevalent on the land. He respected Willie's helplessness, his complete trust and faith in all who cared for him.

But most of all, he coveted the moments when he would gaze into his grandson's eyes. In those eyes, William could see the hope and promise of the future. They seemed to be so full of discernment, of unlimited possibilities, as they drank in all the stimulating sights for the first time.

"This one's no ordinary farmer," he said, predicting the future to no one in particular. "We must be certain that he has all the opportunities available to learn, to study, and to make something of himself."

One Fawcett was not smitten by the new baby. Elizabeth vowed that she would never forgive Rufus for his initial comment when he saw his new nephew. "It certainly is a baby," Rufus had said in an off-handed fashion and then he had gone on about his business. That careless remark had hurt her deeply and she never told her husband or her father what he had said, knowing the chaos it would cause.

However, she never let Willie out of her sight when Rufus was around. She had protected and defended her brother for seventeen years and, in some ways, she was the last to recognize the qualities in him which offended others. But now she, too, was prepared to let him go, to cast him adrift. She no longer trusted him or, in fact, even liked him. He had been hurtful about the most important thing in this new mother's life.

"Mother, I want you to promise me that you will keep your eye on Willie when Rufus is home. I don't want him left alone."

"Dear, I am sure that he...."

Elizabeth cut her off abruptly. "Mother, I mean it." With uncharacteristic forcefulness she persevered. "We will leave immediately, right now, James and Willie and I, if you don't agree to this. It is not open for debate. I do not wish to discuss it further."

Sarah nodded sadly.

Rufus regarded this new baby, this new intrusion, as a delay to his plans. It had never occurred to him while Elizabeth was pregnant, but now he could see clearly what was happening or, rather, what was not happening. James and his sister were not making any plans to move out of the house, his house, in the near future. They were comfortable and his parents seemed to be adjusting to the arrangement and that was not what he had envisioned. It wasn't fair. He knew that it would be years before his father died and left him the farm to do with as he wished. It was his birthright and he wasn't about to wait around and just let things happen. Rufus hatched a scheme to accelerate his ownership of Fawcett farm.

It was Betsy's marriage to James and the subsequent birth of this child that had dashed his hopes and Rufus had seen how much his parents approved of James and enjoyed having him around. As well he saw the love that they squandered on this crying infant. But he also knew the solution. He would get married and, when he and his new bride moved into his home, there wouldn't be enough room for both families so James and Elizabeth and the baby would have to go. It was simple; the farm was his rightfully his by birth, all he had to do was get them all off his land.

This dream rapidly took on a life of its own and began to expand and grow in possibilities. Maybe he and his wife would quickly have a son to establish the rightful heir to the Fawcett fortune. The added bonus to this was the increase in stature and respect and love that a family with grandchildren would give him in his father's eyes. Yes, this all made sense. He could see it happening.

Rufus wasn't blind to his father's attachment to the new grandchild. He had been raised in James's shadow and he could read the signs, he knew them well. At the point that it had seemed that James and Elizabeth might leave so he could enjoy his cycle of basking in his father's favour, along came another to usurp his due and, once again, this one wasn't a real Fawcett either. The one thing that Rufus wanted more than the family money and power was his father's love and approval and that always seemed to allude his grasp or, as Rufus would say, someone else would always steal it.

"Not this time," he vowed.

Chapter XV

Like most plans conceived in the mind of a seventeen year old, this one had some flaws, some serious flaws, that Rufus would be forced to overcome. Although he had been courting the girls of Sackville, he hadn't yet found a steady one whom he might marry, but that little fact didn't stop him. This plan had too many possibilities to be derailed by some small details.

So he went to his usual haunt, the tavern, to mull over his options. He slid onto a bench at a table where his usual drinking buddies were already in their cups but he knew that he would be unable to count on their assistance in this dilemma. As he looked around to place his order, one of the lads asked him, "Are you gettin' any sleep with the wee one cryin' and goin' on all night?"

"From what I've been hearing, sleep ain't all he's not gettin'." This remark brought howls of laughter from the other young men.

"Don't you worry," Rufus responded, "They're soon moving out." Their reminding him of his troubles at home was annoying. After all, that was why he came here in the first place, to escape.

"Sure, Rufus, and the King's setting up residence here in Sackville."

But the banter and jibes of his friends couldn't dislodge his optimism tonight. If only he could find a wife. If only he could get a drink.

Then, like a miracle, the solution to both of his problems walked over to the table. Eliza Cornwall, the barmaid, was there to take his order. She was an attractive young lady who had come from Halifax with her daughter. Twenty-four years of age, Eliza was the victim of a temporary marriage with one of the British soldiers from the garrison there and left to fend for herself and her child when he was relocated. Being disillusioned with soldiers, she had decided to seek her fortune in this town.

That evening Rufus started his relationship with Eliza. So what if she was a little coarse around the edges, she was sexy and good-looking, she was available and she was looking for a husband to provide and care for her.

She liked Rufus. He was fun and he was young and he was cute. That Rufus had some breeding and belonged to a substantial family more than made up for his quirks, his moods and his immaturity. Besides, he was good to her, obviously infatuated by her looks and maturity.

During the following days Rufus spent every possible hour with Eliza. She was careful not to impose her child on the relationship, at least not yet. She knew how to please a man, she knew how to build up a man with praise, she knew how to bring a man along by promises and pledges that activated the imagination but left him coming back for more. A mere boy, like Rufus, was no challenge at all.

When one of the other servers remarked on her new beau, Eliza dismissed it with, "It's like taking candy from a baby and I've got this baby eating out of my hand."

"I'd say that baby is suckling at your teat, and that's no lie," responded her colleague and they both giggled and laughed without the hint of a blush.

Rufus spent more and more time in that particular tavern and wallowed in the obvious attention that she showered on him. None of Rufus's friends said anything bad about his new girl, that was his business and it is doubtful that if they had, he would have listened. So all the patrons ignored his silly flirtings and dallyings.

That is all but one, Jake Oulton. Old Jake was well known around Sackville and although he had no real job, he made certain that he had enough money to buy his rum and some of the other necessities of life. Preferring to earn that money in the easiest fashion possible, Old Jake had found that information was valuable and selling what he knew or could discover was his favourite, least arduous means of making a few shillings. He watched Rufus and Eliza knowing that to someone, somewhere what was happening in this tavern would be worth a drink or two.

On the occasion of James and Elizabeth's first wedding anniversary, William announced that he wanted to talk to the whole family after church on Sunday. Rufus was ecstatic and he could hardly wait to find Eliza for he was sure he knew the purpose of the family gathering. "Darling, father is going to give me the farm. Just think, we'll be set."

"Farm? What do you want a farm for? I don't see you as no farmer. That's not the proper work for a smart man like you, a man of breeding and book learning."

"No, no. Don't you see?" he said impatiently. "I am going to inherit the farm and maybe sell it or maybe hire my brother-in-law to run it and then I'll have it made — money and position."

"Oh, you are so smart," she purred running her tongue around his ear. "You won't leave me then, will you — you all rich and a landowner and the like?" She pouted and added, "We'll have it made — money and position? I fancy being rich and I fancy being made and in any position."

Rufus smiled at her. "That's my Eliza."

When Sunday arrived, Rufus was ready as they all took their places at the pine table. He had gone to church with them that morning which had made Sarah very pleased and he even cooed a cheery welcome to Willie who was lying in his mother's arms. Sitting in the chair at the end of the table opposite to his father he reasoned, "It is my rightful place," and was justifiably excited.

Rufus turned to his brother-in-law. "James, I really like what you and my father have done around here. You have worked hard and the effort shows. The farm is coming along and it is one of the finest pieces of land in New Brunswick."

"Why thank you, Rufus." James thought that just maybe the boy was growing up at last. "I didn't believe that you noticed what went on at the farm."

"Notice? Why James, it is my intention to take a more active part in what goes on around here." Rufus adjusted himself in his chair. "I have been far too busy up to now but things are starting to come together."

"I am so pleased to hear you say that, Rufus." William smiled at his son. "That is exactly what I want to talk to all of you about. It is why I called this family meeting. I am so proud to hear you talk like that."

Rufus swelled with pride. Finally he was getting the recognition that he wanted, that he deserved, from his father. He glanced at his mother but Sarah was staring intently at something on her hand.

William began. "It was a fortuitous day when James came to our farm. You were only two at the time, Rufus, and Betsy was six. He has lived as a member of our family and, I believe, has been treated as a member of our family." Rufus nodded in agreement. "This farm has grown and flourished as we have increased its size. Our breeding program is one to be envied and our crop yield increases each year. This is in a large measure because of you, James, and I thank you for that."

Rufus smiled at James. Yes, he could admit that James had done much more around the farm than could reasonably expected of a hired man.

James looked up from his folded hands and said, "I have received far more than I have given and no thanks are required." He well knew that the purpose of this meeting was to give control of the farm to the son, as was the custom and wondered what that would mean to him and his family, and William and the farm.

William continued, "I have come to think of James as a Fawcett so your marriage made me twice happy. Nothing has given me more joy than the birth of my grandson and, Elizabeth, I thank you for such a beautiful present. Sarah and I have waited to try to find the right wedding gift for you and I think that we have finally agreed on the appropriate choice. Contrary to usual custom, my two children, Elizabeth and Rufus, shall be joint heirs of this property when I die. It will go to both of you."

It might be expected that such an announcement by William would evoke a boisterous response from at least three of the people at the table however, there was silence. There was no noise; it was quiet. It took some time for Rufus and James and Elizabeth to internalize what he had said and then, one at a time, they verified it.

"Joint heirs?"

"Both of us will own the farm?"

"She will own it, too?"

During this whole exchange Sarah had been silent, but her attention had been focused only on Rufus. She now said, "I know this will take you some time to digest the significance of our decision, so why don't we all leave it for now and think over the consequences?"

Later that night, the conversation in three different locales was centered around the same topic.

"Can he do that?" asked Eliza. "I thought it was a law or something that the eldest son got the property. It's not fair."

"I don't think he knows that I've changed, that I am going to settle down. James has made him do this. That bastard ruins everything! I'm certain that my father will give me what is rightfully mine when he thinks it over. James and Elizabeth had this baby just to steal my land."

In the privacy of their bedroom, James and Elizabeth cuddled and whispered their thoughts. "Did you see the look on Rufus's face?" Elizabeth snuggled closer. "I thought he was going to cry."

"It must have come as quite a shock to him. I know it was for me." James stroked her hair. "I feel sorry for Rufus. He feels that nobody loves him, that nobody cares."

"I'm done feeling sorry for my brother. You worked this farm and you deserve to reap the benefits. What has he ever done except cause trouble?"

Meanwhile, in the parlour, William and Sarah were enjoying a cup of tea by the warmth of the fire. "It was the right decision, Sarah. James and Elizabeth helped to make this place and they will continue to improve it."

"I worry about Rufus." Sarah put her cup down and took her husband's rough hands in hers. Rubbing them lightly with her thumbs she looked into his eyes. "I know you are right but he is still young. Maybe with a little more time and understanding...."

"We've been through that many times before. It's no use. He is indeed fortunate that I have consented to give him half."

William put closure on the topic by rising from his chair. "I am going over to John's tomorrow to talk to him and put this to paper."

Adjusting his cap on his unruly hair and brushing at some of the dirt on his jacket, Jake Oulton wiped his sleeve across his mouth. Looking down at his feet, he rubbed the toes up and down the back of his trousers. Breathing in deeply precipitated some more hacking and coughing, but he was ready, he knew he was good at this. It was late when he rapped lightly on the door frame but the door opened a crack allowing the light and warmth to escape.

"Oh, it's you. What do you want?" The gruff manner was not usual from such a gentleman.

The sickly sweet smell of rum preceded the answer, "If you'd be excusin' me for callin' so late, but I believe I might be in the possession of some facts that might be precious to someone as important as yourself."

"Get on with it Jake."

"Well this is information that might be worthy and of value to you, I mean, someone of such a fine family as yours, if you get my meanin'." He coughed up a wad of phlegm and spit it over his shoulder into the grass beside the walk. Wiping his mouth with the back of his worn wool glove, he added, "But if I'm wastin' your time, so to speak, I do rightly apologize and will be on my way."

The gentleman fetched a few shillings from his pocket and held them out as one might do with a bone in front of a dog, withholding the treat until the trick is performed.

"Well you see, Sir, it's young Rufus, you see." Jake paused to catch his breath as the air burned his lungs. "He's been down at the tavern makin' a darn fool of hisself, if you'll pardon my expression, I mean with messin' with Elizer the barmaid and proposin' and such." He paused as he tried to peer over the gentleman's shoulder to catch a glimpse of the world inside. "You see, with him promisin' her the farm and the like, she's not his sort of lady what with the child and all, if you follow my drift."

He had heard enough. John Fawcett paid the money and quickly closed the door. He frowned and bit his lower lip as he wrapped his sweater more tightly around his body and shivered. It had become suddenly cooler in the house. Quickly walking to the basin and pitcher, he poured the water and washed his hands thoroughly.

Jake walked back to the tavern, the coins jingling safely inside his glove. He was proud of himself for the good day's work but he would keep himself aware of the situation for there might be more drinking money to be made.

For the last few days, Rufus had been in the habit of taking out one of the rifles and practicing with it as he found that it gave him a certain amount of relief from the tensions of worrying about the farm. Sometimes he would put an old hat on a stick and prop it up against the fence before he would blast at it. He found his aim improved if he ascribed particular names to the figure. He might have gone hunting and, with the plethora of game about, he would have had more excitement, but Rufus didn't like the idea of killing a defenseless animal. It was hardly sporting.

William returned from John's with a look of resolve on his face. Once more he called the family around the pine table. This time he stood, refusing to sit down.

At first Rufus might have thought that the purpose of this meeting was to restore the farm to its proper heir, but one look at his father quickly dispelled any such notions. He had never seen his father so angry.

"I am not going to have you squander all that I have worked for these sixty-two years. I didn't come from Yorkshire and claw and slave my way at this damnable land for you to flirt about with some trollop, some harlot who wants nothing more than for you to provide for her and her bastard child. Rufus you're a damn fool." None of them had seen William like this, his red face beaded with perspiration despite the coolness of the room. One single vein throbbed visibly in his neck as he bellowed, "You ungrateful child. Have you learned nothing? Did I raise you to be that stupid? Do you think me an imbecile?"

Rufus knew enough than to answer these questions. He felt all cold and clammy as he squirmed and wiggled under the onslaught from his father but he had long ago learned the technique of focusing on other thoughts rather than listening to the bad things that people were saying. How his father had found out about Eliza was a mystery and, although he knew what his father really thought about him, to voice these things in front of the others was pure torture and so unfair. He would never forgive him for this. He would never forgive any of them; they'd be sorry.

"You have no intentions of farming, do you? You don't intend to learn farming, do you? Did you think that you would take all this that others have worked so hard for and squander it? Do you honestly think that I would let you do that? Are you an idiot?"

James dared not look up from the table. He was mortified for poor Rufus, but to whatever William was alluding, it must be serious. Elizabeth was ashamed — ashamed that her brother would treat her father so and bring him to this. Sarah sat absolutely still, the tears running down her cheeks. Why couldn't the two of them allow for each other? But she knew better than to interfere.

"I sat here at this very table, not a week ago, and announced the division of this farm. I am going to tell you right now, that is not a certainty." William paused. Rufus held his breath. "Unless there are some rather significant changes around here, I may decide to dispose of my property differently." Spreading his arms apart, he said, "James and Elizabeth might get all this and you, my ungrateful son, nothing. Now get out of my sight."

Rufus pulled on his new, expensive boots, wrapped himself in his black topcoat and headed out into the night. He was confused and humiliated as he walked slowly to town. That damn worker had stole his father, had stole his sister was now about to steal his farm. He fussed and fumed as he paced down the road his mind whirling and spinning as he considered the possibilities. It was that damn brat, that bawling child, Willie. He must do something. He thought of his father with all his money and his power, lording it over him. He thought of James enjoying the position and love which were rightly his. God he hated him.

He had always been able to think his way through problems and come up with a plan, a workable solution and as he approached the tavern, it came to him. He knew what he must do.

Rufus sat at his accustomed table, surrounded by his friends. One of them nudged his elbow, "You're deep in thought tonight. What has caused this mood?"

Rufus sipped his brandy, staring straight ahead without a smile. "I've learned a bit today. If you want something to happen you have to make it happen." He slammed the glass down on the table.

"What in bloody hell is that supposed to mean?" asked one of the lads. They were used to his moods.

"He means like if you want a drink, you've got to yell like this, 'Give me a drink'." This brought fits of laughter and back-pounding at the table.

Still Rufus was serious. "My father used to say, 'Like the weather, times are going to change and just as fiercely but without as much warning.'" He then announced loudly, "He'll see. You'll all see. There is going to be a great overturn in the

Fawcett household. Mark my words." He then rose, drained his glass and left with Eliza close behind.

The usual jokes and repartee stopped for a moment while the friends thought over what he had said. Then they began talking excitedly.

"What does he mean by that?"

"Well I guess he intends to up and marry Eliza."

"And take her home to his father? I'd like to see that. The boy has bigger balls than that bull of theirs."

"I heard him say that he was going to marry Eliza and that they were going to move into the Fawcett place."

"And do what?"

"Manage the place."

"Rufus a farmer? Listen to what you're saying."

"Come on. Eliza a farmer's wife?"

"I'm just telling you what I heard."

Rufus trudged home. The trip to the tavern had not changed his mind. If anything, it had solidified things, and made him more confident of what he must do.

Chapter XVI

During the middle of June, 1832, the weather in New Brunswick was unseasonably warm. The sun was shining brightly with not a cloud in the sky so William and James chose to use this beautiful day to their advantage to check the honey bees.

Like most farms, they kept bees to provide the sweetening that they needed and craved, because the honey was cheaper and more readily available than sugar and, to most tastes, more delicious. Much was said about the healing properties of honey so it was often present in remedies and elixirs or given on its own. Mothers administered a spoonful of honey to children with sore throats or colds or with a case of the grippe. Farmers with rheumatism swore by a measure of honey in their tea to provide relief. Honey mixed with equal parts of bee pollen was thought to halt aging. As Grandma Holmes had been fond of saying, "Honey is good for whatever ails you."

On a warm day, a greater number of bees were likely out of the hive collecting nectar from the clover and the golden rod, so it was a good opportunity to check the hives. By this examination, they would know that everything was proceeding well with no rodents nesting in the boxes. A quick look would verify that the frames were being filled with honey and allow them to discover whether the hive needed another super, or box of frames.

James wore the netting that would protect his face from any angry stings although he preferred to work with bare hands, claiming that the gloves were too cumbersome and they angered the bees. When Elizabeth asked about the pain of the occasional sting, James replied that it didn't exactly hurt but, when a bee stings you, still the tendency is to jump and say "damn".

William had prepared the smoker which was a round metal cylinder with a bellows attached. In the smoker he placed some smoldering dry grass. Consequently, when James approached the first hive and gave the bellows a couple of squeezes, he forced puffs of acrid, gray smoke into the entrance to calm the inhabitants.

However, concerned by the few bees flying in the vicinity, he quickly used his hive tool to pry his way inside the cover. What James saw, caused his heart to sink. He had expected to view thousands of the small insects crawling over the frames, instead, there were scarcely a hundred. He pulled up each frame examining it carefully until he saw what he had been dreading, the large sac-like cell, about as big as a thumb, hanging there — a swarm cell.

For whatever reason, the bees in that hive had decided to replace the queen. Instead of hatching the usual worker and drone bees, they had fed the developing larvae a special mixture to produce a queen, probably several queens. Fights to the finish would ensue until only one queen prevailed, usually one of the new, young royals. She would then lead all of the bees, thousands and thousands, out of their hive to find a new home most likely in a hollow tree, old stump or the eaves of a barn. They would set up the new household, miles from this hive, where the honey would be unavailable to William and his family. The handful of bees that were left in the hive had hatched after the swarm and were useless without a queen inasmuch as they did not have the ability to produce another queen — only a queen could do that.

This swarming, in itself, wasn't that unusual. Every couple of years a hive would swarm, for one reason or another. However, what he found as he checked each one of the six hives was that every one of them had swarmed. This never happened and neither he nor William had seen, much less heard, of such a thing. This year they would collect no honey from their hives and both of them had an uneasy feeling that as well this was a portent of bad luck.

Sarah tried to make light of this aberration at supper that night when she said, "We are fortunate that we are living in New Brunswick in this modern age. In other times and in other places they would have called this an omen and branded us all as witches to be burned at the stake." They dropped the topic, but the significance of the bee event left everyone thinking.

Rufus, who had been brooding and excessively quiet since the confrontation with his father, had been spending more time than usual with the family. He was often present for meals and often sat with them well into the evening. He said little and interacted not at all and as much as his presence pleased Sarah, she was enough of a realist to wonder how long it would last. For now, everyone was getting along.

As they were all chatting in the parlour, they heard the sound of a single horse's hooves coming up the path to the house. Sarah remarked, "Who can that be? It's almost seven o'clock." Visits from neighbours were quite common, but not this late in the evening. The whole family crowded to the windows to discover who was coming up the lane in a horse and buggy.

"It's Will and he has somebody with him." James hurriedly opened the door and in burst Will with Martha Chappell and the two were grinning from ear to ear. Martha, a girl of twenty-five years of age, was from Baie Verte and was a cousin of Edward Chappell who had married Will's sister, Eleanor. They knew and liked her.

William took charge. "Will come in here and sit down." He ushered Will to the large pine table. "Get this man a drink, James." The niceties fulfilled, the men looked expectantly at Will while the ladies bunched together in the kitchen. They could tell by his face that it was good news.

Finally William asked, "Well?"

"Uncle, we are on our way home and had to stop and tell you the news. Martha and I are getting married, in August."

Everyone began talking at once.

"That is great news."

"Congratulations Will."

"We are so happy for the two of you."

"Martha is a great girl."

James pumped his arm and vowed, "Now it is my turn to repay you for certain pranks before my wedding." They laughed together.

Will had been disconsolate for quite awhile after the death of Alice so to hear this good news and see him in such high spirits was exhilarating to the others. His wide smile and the quick glances in Martha's direction told the others all they needed to know about his feelings. The next few minutes were filled with questions about how they met, the arrangements, who knew, and the wedding plans. Will and Martha fielded these with excitement.

Will was obviously exploding with happiness and eager to finish the trip to his own house to talk to his father and his wife, Emily. "James. Why don't you and Betsy come with us to talk to father. We can have a few pours and maybe make a party out of it. The night is young."

Elizabeth looked doubtful, "I don't know Will. We have Willie to look after and everything."

"Go on," Sarah interjected. "He's down for the night. Your father and I are quite capable of watching him. Go. Have a good time."

"Not tonight," James declined, "We'll celebrate another night."

As Will and Martha hurried on their way, they were all smiling. James would think back to this moment and speculate that had they gone with Will and Martha, that night may have turned out differently.

"Isn't that great news." Sarah put her hand on top of Elizabeth's. "I have been so worried about Will and those four wee children. Now they will have a mother and Will, a companion. He deserves some good fortune and Martha is perfect for him."

William nodded in agreement. "John and Emily will be very pleased, I know. I think the prospect of helping to raise those four grandchildren was beginning to play on his mind." This statement brought laughter from the family as they imagined Uncle John with Will's family.

"Life has been pretty good to us. Elizabeth, the absolute joy and happiness that you and James and Willie have brought me make my life fulfilled and complete. As I look at all of you, I know that the forecast and the outlook for our farm are good. When I consider how far we have come since our emigration from Yorkshire...." The rest of the words remained unspoken. Each of them let their minds drift to what was important to them. Only Rufus had a frown on his face.

Rufus said absolutely nothing for this last exchange had suddenly made it all clear. He silently observed this cheery family scene as a visitor to a foreign country might and realized that it was he who didn't belong, it was he who wasn't one of them. Finally he comprehended the truth that everyone else had grasped, he was the stranger, the interloper. He was not the future of the farm, the family, the Fawcetts. His father was relying for James for all these things and this had been the design since James had forced himself upon his family sixteen years ago. Rufus was at once enlightened and enraged.

Rufus stood up. He had to get out of there. He had things to do. "It's almost dusk. I'd like to stay but I think that some of our pigs and cattle are down in the marsh again. I think that I'll take the mare and ride down there and see if I can't drive them away."

Sarah protested, "It's eight o'clock at night and it's a good hour's ride there and an hour's ride back. It'll soon be dark."

"When did you suddenly become so interested in farming?" Elizabeth demanded. There was a fair amount of sarcasm in her tone.

"I can't win. You're after me when I don't help and you criticize me when I do."

William said, "Enough. Be on your way then. See if you can make it back for devotions at ten. James and I will finish up in the barn while you're gone."

None of the family was really sorry to see Rufus leave as his absence would make the rest of the evening more enjoyable for all of them. Rufus knew that but now he didn't care.

As they headed to the barn for the rest of the chores, James stared at William. He obviously had been pleased with Will's news since family was so important to him. His love for Elizabeth was limitless and it was obvious how he felt about Willie. James had never heard him speak a strong word to Sarah and from the beginning, William had treated him like a son.

He grabbed a bridle from the peg and ran his fingers over the oiled leather and held it to his nose briefly. He loved the smell — the horsy leather smell.

Why couldn't William and Rufus call a truce? What was it about Rufus that made it impossible for William to love him? William seemed to have boundless amounts of love but the two were like two stags, butting heads and locking antlers. Once, when he had questioned Elizabeth about it, she had responded that they were too much alike — each proud, each unyielding, each arrogant in his own way.

"I said, 'Pass me that shovel.'" James wondered how long he had been dreaming while William was working. He glanced at the elder Fawcett but he continued cleaning the stalls, although James thought that he could detect a slight smile on his face.

Back at the house, James sat at William's place with two long strands of leather running the length of the long pine table. He worked busily with an awl, marking out holes for a new pair of reins. He could hear Elizabeth and Sarah bathing the baby while William fussed with the fire, teasing one of the dogs with a piece of kindling.

He decided that these were his favourite times, the chores all done and the day winding down. He loved to sit and listen to the others chatting back and forth. He felt very much at peace; it was so quiet. He loved his wife and child, the Fawcetts, this farm — not bad for an orphan.

"Did you say something, James?"

Startled he looked up at William. William had brought a candle over to the table for the evening devotions. This was a regular event, every night at ten o'clock William would either read one of Wesley's sermons or a passage from the Bible. They would pray together before they would retire to bed. He enjoyed this time of quiet reflection spent together each night and decided that this was a tradition that he and Elizabeth would carry on when William and Sarah were gone. James shook his head. Again he was brooding too much, thinking too much.

Beginning to rise to vacate William's chair as the others gathered around, William pushed down on his shoulder. "God can hear me just as well from here." He sat down in James's usual spot.

William always read by candle light, never using the lantern. James agreed that the candle gave off such a warm, sleepy glow and he listened to the soothing resonance of William's voice as he read to them. William was always the one who read, never Sarah or Elizabeth or him.

When they had finished reading from the sermons and each had added his own prayer, they sat in silence. James looked at William's large, worn hands — hands that were strong enough to lift a fence rail while tender enough to deliver a calf. He was reading his Bible silently, which was how he always ended this time.

James glanced at Sarah and she had picked up her knitting. He thought of Will and Martha. Sarah now had a purpose for the afghan that she was knitting. He was always amazed by the look of strength in Sarah's eyes for she was an amazing woman and Elizabeth had inherited these traits.

William's head nodded forward. James smiled. This wouldn't be the first time that he had fallen asleep after devotions. Peace. Quiet. What were these little pieces of glass that were showering all over them? Like tiny beads from a broken necklace, they tumbled and rolled, and glinted in the light, resembling winter snow flakes as they fell on their heads, their clothes, the table, the knitting, and the Bible. James gazed curiously at them, not sure what he was seeing.

He threw up his arms so that they were shielding his eyes while at the same time he ducked his head to gain some protection — it would have been too late by this time had he any control over these actions but his moves were instinctive.

Next was the crash — probably the crash was first but it was now that the noise registered. Not a huge explosion, nothing deafening, rather like a muffled pop followed by breaking glass. Familiar with this sound he thought perhaps someone had broken a tea cup.

Then there was the cool air on the back of his neck. His brain was sifting through the myriad of possibilities. He looked over his shoulder to see if the door was ajar but it was closed.

The smell of good times filled his nostrils, days of hunting, the pursuit, the chase, gun powder — the aroma of guns shooting, animals dying — pleasant times with William.

His gaze drifted over to William, but he hadn't moved a muscle. James's mind was racing now. What had happened? He could feel his heart beating wildly in his chest. It was only then that he looked back over his shoulder and noticed the broken kitchen window. So that was what had caused the noise, the glass, the cool air.

James started to rise. He looked back at William; he still hadn't moved. His head was bowed, he must be asleep. The dogs were scrambling over the wood floor, their claws unable to gain a purchase in the smooth pine. They knew better than that. What had gotten into them?

He started to look towards the baby's room and then snapped his head back to stare at William. Something was not right. That red on his shirt. He hadn't noticed that before and it was growing from a scarlet speck to a crimson spot. His eyes were riveted to the stain as it slowly spread, expanding larger and larger, seeping slowly from one fibre to the next, oozing sluggishly outward. Transfixed, he was unable to react and unable to move. How pretty the mark looked. How long would it take to cover his whole shirt?

Then came the screams, not short screams of fright but long, prolonged screams, more like wails. He had heard screams like that from the rabbits before they died in the snares. At first he hadn't believed that rabbits make noises, but they do and that is how they sounded. He listened while the screams pierced the blackness of the New Brunswick night and spread from the peaceful house, out across the quiet fields and pastures, down the silent lane, through the noiseless woods and over the tranquil marshes to be lost in the bay and the ocean beyond. They seemed to roll on and on for eternity.

Then, as abruptly as they had begun, they stopped. James looked up. This had all happened in a matter of seconds though James could visualize each separate detail, thought and emotion for in that moment of infinity, time had stood absolutely still forever in that farm house.

James willed himself to move, to act, to speak. "Elizabeth, look after your mother." James reached across and shook her. "Elizabeth. Elizabeth. Do as I say. Take your mother into our bedroom. Now! Check the baby."

He reached across and felt William's neck. Nothing. He put his hand on William's chest and then suddenly recoiled from the sticky, warm syrup staining his fingers. Frantically he wiped his hand down the leg of his pants and, for some odd reason, he stopped and smelled his hand. He drew back quickly and felt sick.

He ran outside to the porch and groped about until he grasped the metal bar in his hand. He stuck it inside the triangle of iron and, with all his strength, he forced his arm to whirl around in frenzied circles. He rang and he banged and he clanged until he thought that the sound would shatter his eardrums. Then, standing still, he listened.

Moving again, he rushed back inside just as Sarah emerged from the bedroom with Elizabeth trying to drag her back by the arm. It was difficult for him to understand what he was seeing. Elizabeth's yells were mixed with sobs. "Mother, no. Mother, you can't."

Sarah strode forward, a purpose to her walk. She stared directly at William. She bent down over him, gazed sternly at his face and said, "William, don't you die. You can't... I can't." She bent down and, tilting his head up, she tearlessly kissed him softly on the lips.

Sarah collapsed into a motionless heap at William's feet. Among the garble of other thoughts, each realized that life would never be the same. Confused and bewildered James stared at the figure in the chair. Then it became clear and his thoughts were bombarded by the stark realization — William was sitting in his chair. It was meant to be he, not William, who was dead.

Chapter XVII

A most atrocious Murder has been committed in this hitherto peaceful part of the country. On Tuesday evening last, Mr. William Fawcett, living in the upper part of this parish called his family together about 10 o'clock to attend their evening devotion, which being over, he was sitting by a candle reading his Bible, when some monster in human shape fired a gun through the window at him and killed him immediately; he never spoke nor moved after being shot. Mr. Fawcett was a man of most amiable character, mild, inoffensive and retiring in his manners; he probably never willfully offended any person; and has died universally regretted by all who knew him.

New Brunswick Royal Gazette
July 4, 1832

The alarm that James had rung was common in one form or another to every home in this area. It was not used to call the men for supper or to tell the children that it was time to come home or for any of the other everyday incidents. It meant one thing and one thing only — help. If you can hear this alarm, come running and everybody did. It might be a fire or an accident, but one thing was certain, it was an emergency.

Within minutes, the neighbours were crowding into the Fawcett house. Joseph Sears and his son Frederick were the first to arrive, Joseph sent Frederick to get Dr. Nathaniel Smith and then covered up William's body with a blanket. Thomas and Ruth Weaton and Robert and Edith Emmerson were next; Ruth and Edith took charge of Sarah and Elizabeth and the baby, while Thomas and Robert huddled with James in the corner. "Long" John Thompson and his sons, Wilson and Jacob headed out on horseback to find Sheriff Chandler. Tolar Thompson and his cousin Joseph joined forces with Woodworth, the blacksmith, and George Lawrence and his sons, Nathan and Leban, and organized the rest of the men to do a thorough search of the outside to see if they could find the perpetrator or any clues to his identity. The women belonging to these men, cleaned up the mess and began making coffee and tea and gathering food for what could prove to be a long night. The rest of the neighbours and friends gathered on the porch and began the talk.

"Who would want to kill William?"

"That man didn't offend a person in this world."

"Imagine, a shooting in Sackville."

"I'd like to have my squirrel rifle and seen the man who done it."

"What's the sense of it. William wouldn't harm nobody."

And so it went, around and around, but the consensus was one of absolute shock at the event and the victim.

Within the half hour, Sheriff Charles Chandler arrived. Charles Chandler was a son of Joshua Chandler, a prominent loyalist and a fifth generation American. He came from a family that made a career out of law enforcement in a rugged and difficult land and nobody messed with Sheriff Chandler.

For one thing, he was big — he stood well over six feet and weighed something over two hundred pounds. Secondly, it was well known that you never win an argument with Sheriff Chandler. People who knew said that if you began to get the better of him, he'd hit you; he'd hit you with whatever was handy. From time to time he was known to use a chair, a stone bottle, a stick, a rock or his fist to subdue a drunk or enforce any law that he felt was worth enforcing at the time. He was a good sheriff if you were on the right side of the law.

Before the Sheriff had time to say anything, Johnnie and Will arrived. They quickly found James and pressed him for the details.

Close on their heals was Dr. Nathaniel Smith. Dr. Smith was one of the most respected doctors in the area. He was the representative for Westmorland in the Assembly, but first and foremost he was a doctor. He was short and stocky and not at all anybody's image of a doctor or a parliamentarian. He had an annoying habit of peering over his spectacles whether he was reading a paper or giving a diagnosis.

Sheriff Chandler immediately took charge.

"All right now," Chandler's voice boomed, "If you know anything or saw anything stay out on the porch, otherwise go home. That goes for you, too, Ed. Now get out of here. You aren't helping." Nobody moved.

Turning to Thomas Ayer, he said, "Tom, take that lamp and go outside the kitchen window and check for footprints or anything else. Mind where you step. If you see anything just stand still and don't let anybody else near. Understand?"

The Sheriff turned and looked over his shoulder as the sound of uncontrolled sobbing came from the bedroom. "She's taking it pretty bad and I can't say I blame her but the best thing we can do is find the person who did this." He didn't say this to anyone in particular but everyone in the room nodded in agreement.

"Dr. Smith, I know you are just home from the Assembly, but you're a doctor and not a bad one at that." Actually this was high praise from Sheriff Chandler. "I'd be obliged if you'd look at the body and then see to Mrs. Fawcett and Elizabeth."

Drawing John and James and Will into a corner away from the lifeless form of William Fawcett, Chandler removed his hat and wiped his brow, "Now we haven't got much so far. All we know is William was shot once in the chest. Killed him dead. Anyone of you know someone who'd have reason to want Mr. Fawcett dead?"

James scarcely heard the question. His mind was still back reliving the horror of the crime. The irony of fortune had not escaped him. "It should have been me," he sobbed, "He was sitting in my chair tonight. Except for those reins, they would have killed me. They should have killed me. Why? Why would they do this?"

The Sheriff thought it odd that James would say "they", but decided to let it pass, for now. He turned to John Fawcett who in this moment looked older and grayer.

John shook his head. "Charles, you knew William. Everybody liked him. He didn't have any enemies." He closed his hands in fists, trying desperately to remain in control. He lowered his voice. "He was a peace-loving man. He went to church. Why would someone do this? What's the purpose? What does it accomplish?"

"I know. I liked William, too." He paused, looked around and asked, "Any debts? Anybody owe him money? Things going well with the missus?"

"Come on Chandler," John was angry now. "You know better than that. Maybe if you stopped asking damn fool questions and...."

"I know, I know, but I've got to ask. It's my job. I don't like this any better than you do. Now you two see to your ladies. We'll find who did this and the gallows will be too good for them."

Sheriff Chandler was looking around the room wondering what to do next, when Rufus Fawcett walked into the house. Rufus did not barge in, he did not burst in, he did not even hurry in, he walked in. His face was impassive. He was placid and calm. It was as if he were coming home for supper.

"Hello. What's going on? Why's everybody here?"

When they informed Rufus that his father had been murdered, his reply was "Have the Indians killed my father?" He said it so calmly, almost as a statement rather than a question. It was so absurd a response, so ridiculous an accusation that no one answered. They all just stood and stared at Rufus. No one could believe it. One or two even said the word out loud, "Indians?", before a word or a nudge in the ribs shushed them.

His reactions were so different from anyone in the house, that every person who was present that night remarked on it. It was something about his manner, his responses, his walk, his voice, his whole demeanor that seemed odd. Right from the first, he showed none of the surprise, the indignation, the shock, the anger, the outrage, the confusion, the offense, the consternation, the trauma, the horror that one would expect the son of a murder victim to show — the responses that every person in that house, save Rufus, was demonstrating. It was strange, very strange.

Moreover, Rufus did not say or ask those things that a loving and devoted son is supposed to say or ask. He did not rant or rave or demand answers or demand justice or promise retribution. He didn't cry or yell or even raise his voice. He was cool and serene, reserved and contained.

As John Goodall said later, "It wouldn't at all have surprised me if he had let out a big yawn and then gone over to the larder and looked for one of Sarah's shortbread cookies."

If these actions weren't enough, when Rufus heard some of the neighbours expressing shock at his behaviour and disbelief at what he had said, he further compounded the problem. He called out, "I do not care what any person thinks." Again, as one, the neighbours turned and stared and shook their heads not wanting to accept what they had heard. How the son of murdered William Fawcett could behave like this was beyond their comprehension.

As an attempt to prevent Rufus from further embarrassing himself, Sheriff Chandler decided to draw him aside and ask him a few questions. These were not accusations as Rufus was not a suspect. They were questions to try and see if the boy knew or saw anything.

"Rufus, I know you are upset, but I want to ask you a few things. This is an awful affair and we are all deeply shocked." However, Rufus did not look deeply shocked, or even just plain shocked, for that matter. "Where were you tonight?"

This was a simple query that anyone there could answer with very little difficulty. It wasn't supposed to be hard. However it might as well have been a difficult mathematical equation or a question in a foreign language.

"Me? Well I was here all the time." Rufus stammered. "I mean I went out for awhile, but nowhere special. I was here but I just went out for, ah, a walk for a bit."

"Now take it easy, son. Settle down. Were you here or not?"

"Well, yes. I mean, no. I was out with some friends"

"All right. Who were your friends?" He paused but there was no response. "The ones that you were out with?"

"Who? I don't remember their names. They were just friends."

By this time all those listening began to feel uncomfortable. Some turned away or shuffled their feet or looked at their neighbours, but they couldn't stop listening.

"We all went to the tavern."

"Now what tavern was that?" asked the Sheriff.

James, like the rest of the neighbours, was listening to this exchange. He was aghast. He had never before seen Rufus like this. He must be confused. "Rufus. Don't you remember? You rode down to the far marsh to chase home the cattle."

Rufus looked slightly relieved. "Of course. I was just a little bit mixed up there. That's where I was. I rode down to the far marsh."

There was a collective sigh of relief. It had been like watching some moron, some incompetent, trying to accomplish some difficult task that was far too complex and finally, he had done it. At least that was cleared up.

Chandler continued, "Now, what time did you leave here?"

"Eight o'clock," answered Rufus. He nodded. "Yes, eight o'clock." James nodded his assent and soon everyone was nodding, as if to encourage the young lad.

"So, it's about an hour down to the marsh and an hour back plus time to find the animals." Everyone was doing the calculations. The Sheriff looked at his pocket watch, "And you're just getting back now which works out about right, I'd say."

Again everyone relaxed slightly. Chandler removed his hat and began scratching again. As if on cue, George Lawrence entered holding a rifle. "Sheriff, look what we found over the fence in the garden at the Sears place."

Charles Chandler took the rifle gingerly and held it up to his nose. He worked the mechanism and a spent shell flew out of the breach. Bending down, he picked it up, looked at it and slipped it into his pocket. As if evaluating the rifle before deciding on whether to make a purchase, he stroked the length of the barrel, squinted down the sights, and then placed his finger into the barrel. Removing his finger, he looked at it before rubbing the result on his pant leg.

He offered the rifle to Rufus asking, "Ever seen this gun before?"

Rufus took the gun and turned it over and over in his hands, as if had never before handled a firearm. He handed it back.

"No. It's not a gun that I recognize. I don't know much about guns. I don't know who that one belongs to."

Chandler handed the gun to James who examined it quickly. He whispered something to John Fawcett and handed it back.

The Sheriff retrieved the shell casing from his pocket and flipped it nonchalantly between his fingers and held it out to Rufus. "What about this? Do you know anyone who uses this type of ammunition?"

Rufus looked at it casually and answered, "No." The Sheriff passed it to James who just shrugged and passed it back.

"Rufus do you use guns? Have you fired a gun lately?"

"I can't remember the last time that I fired a gun, Sheriff. I am not much of a hunter. It must be two months now since I've had a gun in my hands."

Chandler ran his hand over his face as if checking to see if it was time for a shave.

"What about plinking? Target shooting?"

"Never."

Several of the neighbours looked at each other, but no one said anything. Still James stared at the floor.

"Hmmm." Chandler rubbed his eyes. "I think the rest of you better go home now." He stretched out his arms wide as one does before a big yawn.

"What about Thomas?" asked Frederick Sears.

Chandler looked around the room in confusion. "Thomas?"

Sears responded, "Thomas Ayer. He has some footprints outside the kitchen window and says that you told him to stand guard and not move if he found anything."

The Sheriff smiled and, picking up a candle, he went outside. He was back in a couple of minutes. "James, Rufus, give me your left boot and give me William's, too."

James and Rufus retired to the parlour and sat gazing at the fire. James looked into Rufus's face, staring at him but Rufus didn't look flustered or concerned. James wasn't sure what he expected to see, but Rufus appeared to be completely in control of himself and of the situation. As John and Will came over and sat with them, James compared what he saw in their faces with what he saw in Rufus's face.

He thought to himself, how little we know about what really goes on inside a person. How little we know about what really makes a person tick, their fears, their desires, their feelings, their secrets. Less than two hours ago, he had been talking to William and now he was gone. Dead. He should have been able to prevent it. It was his fault. It was meant to be him. He bowed his head in shame.

"Sarah and Elizabeth are going to need your boys' strength," Johnnie sighed. "We'll help any way that we can."

That was the moment that James realized that he had to go on. It was up to him now. William would have wanted it that way, he had brought him up that way. He couldn't be moping and feeling sorry for himself.

The Sheriff came back inside and placed the boots by the door as Dr. Smith handed him something and whispered to him. Chandler examined the object in his hand and looked back over to where the Rufus was sitting. He looked down at his feet and kicked at something imaginary on the floor.

With a look of resignation he walked over to the parlour and asked, "I wonder if you would show me where William keeps his guns." It was a command more than a question.

"They're in that locked chest," replied Rufus, "but I don't know where he keeps the key."

James could feel his heart flip in his chest as he wanted to go over and smash the boy. His arm and chest muscles tightened as he fought to regain control. With a frown he got the key and opened the chest for the Sheriff, who looked inside at the two rifles. He picked up the shell box, examined the shells and then shut the lid.

Suddenly he turned to James and asked, "William kept his guns in good condition? All three of them?"

"Of course he did." James couldn't understand why he would ask such a silly question. "He was very particular about the firearms and such. Kept them all cleaned and oiled."

Chandler reached into his pocket once more and retrieved the slug and the casing. He turned to Rufus and said "Rufus, you said that you have never seen shells like this. Look at them again. These ones came from William's gun chest."

Rufus looked indifferent. "Those? Yes, those are my father's shells. Yes, we have slugs like that."

"Now Charles," interrupted John, "Don't you think we have had enough for one night? Maybe you could continue this tomorrow and just leave us in peace now. My brother has been killed and his widow is in the other room. We're all pretty upset. I've got to see to her and we have some talking to do." He stood up as if to dismiss the big man.

Charles reached into his back pocket and removed a large dirty handkerchief with which he proceeded to wipe his forehead. He stopped and looked at each of the men slowly, seemed to take in a deep breath and then let it out carefully.

"I'm leaving this boy in your hands," he said nodding at Rufus, "But things don't look good." Now turning his complete attention to the boy, he said, "Rufus, I want you to stick around here. I am afraid that there is going to be a Coroner's Inquest and after that, well, I don't know what might happen." He was about to say something else but instead, he shook his head, turned and left.

James felt the colour drain from his face, the perspiration dripping under his arms, the lump rising in his throat. He coughed and ran his fingers through his hair. He wanted to get up and run; he wanted to run to Elizabeth and have her hug him and kiss his face and tell him that everything was going to be all right; he wanted to run and grab his baby, their baby and hold him tightly.

John Fawcett sank back into the chair, his face white and cold. He put his hand to his left breast as if to slow his heart. His head dropped into his hands while his shoulders shook with silent sobs. He thought of the things that he had said and those that he hadn't said and he wished that there had been more time.

Will looked up and out the window, the magic of this night and his wedding announcement shattered. He glanced around at all the familiar objects which had been a part of his uncle and now were once again, just objects. He saw his books, his pipe, the chair, the whole house — they were all William.

Only Rufus looked the same. He sat quietly with a calm look on his face, he might have been waiting to be called for supper. There appeared to be no emotion, no response. Only once did he frown slightly and say, "When he says that I've got to stick around here, I can go down to the tavern, can't I?"

The other three men kept looking at the floor.

Chapter XVIII

During the investigation by the Coroner's Jury, Rufus behaved exactly the same as he had on the night of the murder — he did not exhibit any emotion or any concern. When Dr. Nathaniel Smith presented his testimony, describing the state of the body, the entrance wound, and other details, all listened in horror, often covering their mouths or sobbing or crying or gasping in disbelief at the grisly testimony. Men and women who were accustomed to death by war, or disease, or accident — as common as death was in the 1832 in this brutal land — froze in silence not able to convince themselves, not wanting to accept what they were hearing. When Sheriff Chandler told of his findings, his discoveries, his investigations, even those who had little use for the law turned away and wondered how this could happen in their peaceful, little town. Moreover, those who knew and respected this family of Yorkshire settlers who were prominent, respected, well-liked members of New Brunswick, were unable to fathom how this atrocity could possibly involve the Fawcetts. Still, from Rufus there was no sentiment and no worry.

The evidence was overwhelming and the decision was obvious, no one expected anything any different. Rufus Fawcett was to stand trial for the murder of his father, William Fawcett. The trial would take place when the circuit court came to Sackville in September. It was only then, when it was announced that Rufus was to be taken away to jail that he exhibited any feelings as he moved his head in incredulity and, some said, he shed a few tears. Even that little act on his part seemed more congruent with someone telling him that today was a holiday and that the public house would be closed than with his incarceration, trial and sentencing.

Attending this inquest was a torture to Sarah, but she insisted on being present for every minute. During the whole procedure she cried and she cried hard; she mourned and wept openly both for her husband and for the fate of her son.

"I saw her fondling one of father's sweaters," whispered Elizabeth. "Last night she held one of his shirts to her face and sat there smelling it. She just sat there motionless, with a strange, faraway smile on her face. I had to leave. It tore me up inside."

"Did you notice your father's place set at the supper table? It was all there — knife, fork, plates, his cup — as if she expected him to be home any minute. I didn't say anything, I just put them away."

Sometimes they saw her look up from her knitting as if to share a private thought or special story with her husband. Sarah was much like the dogs who, more often than was usual, would pop up their heads expectantly at the slightest noise, awaiting the return of their master.

Suddenly this behaviour stopped. As the Coroner's Inquest announced its decision she ended her mourning. She made it known that she wanted no more sympathetic visits from friends and neighbours — no more meals prepared and left at the door. Bundling up all William's clothes, she dumped them on the table instructing James that what he wouldn't wear, she would use for rags. William's books and papers were sent over to Johnnie with a note of appreciation for all his kindness. That night at supper she revealed the new seating plan for meals and insisted that James sit at the head of the table in William's seat. She dispersed his valuables, gracing James with the book of Wesley's sermons.

The one item they all wondered about was his favourite chair to the right of the hearth. Each had his own private memory of William sitting in it, dosing or reading or visiting or talking. No one had dared sit there since his death but Sarah solved the problem. She rearranged the furniture and sent for Will to whom she gave the chair as a wedding present saying that Uncle William would have wanted it that way.

On July 24, the administration of William Fawcett's estate was granted to James George, William Crane, and John Fawcett. Johnnie and Will and William Birnham were directed to appraise the estate. This was the legal part. Sarah had already sat down with Johnnie and James and Elizabeth and Will and had spread open the books of the accounts with the decree that James was to carry on the everyday workings of the farm until further notice. When John began to protest, she added that, for now, she would handle the finances and the others were to expedite this to the best of their abilities. The implied threat was "or she would know the reason why."

James turned over in bed to lean on his elbow while he brushed Elizabeth's hair out of her face. "Your mother is amazing. She is so strong, so resourceful. I don't know how she goes on like this."

"Because she has to." Elizabeth paused to let this sink in. It was all so clear to her. "What else is she going to do? Should she just quit? Roll over and die? It doesn't work that way; life goes on."

"I know, but she deserves better than this." He was no longer shocked by Elizabeth's black and white appraisal of circumstances.

"James, you're like her; you're the same. Look what you have endured. It's no different. None of us can sit down and draw out the plan for the life we would like to live. Maybe it's better this way."

"No, Elizabeth, I think you're more like her. It's so simple to you. What does she think about Rufus? Does she think he did it?"

"God, James. Don't be so naive. Don't you understand? It doesn't matter whether he did it or not. William was her husband but Rufus is her son. She will support him, she must support him, regardless. It has nothing to do with what he did or whom he did it to."

"Well, maybe he won't be found guilty. The trial hasn't begun yet and anything can happen."

Elizabeth laughed. It had been awhile since he had heard her laugh spontaneously like that. It sounded good again.

"Uncle Johnnie used to call father 'the optimist'. I think that you are taking over that role. You have already heard some of the evidence and more is bound to come out. You have heard people talking, you know what they're saying. You have seen Rufus, the way he is behaving, the way he is acting. What do you think?"

James kissed away the tear that was rolling down Elizabeth's cheek. "How do you feel about your brother?"

"I don't honestly know. Ask me again when the trial is over." With that they turned away from each other to think their own thoughts and to feel their own feelings.

John came over to their house the next evening and sat with Sarah at the table, while James and Elizabeth played with Willie in the parlour.

"Have you seen him?" he asked. "How is he taking it?"

"Much the same, Johnnie. I take him food every day." Sarah's shoulders rose as she breathed in and then gradually lowered as she tried to relax. She repositioned a strand of hair that had stubbornly fallen over her eyes. There appeared to be more lines on her brow than he remembered. "He is back to the way he was before the inquest, like nothing matters, like nothing will happen. What are we going to do?"

"It doesn't look good, Sarah. I won't deceive you about that. He has done nothing to help himself, nothing to clear himself. Some are painting gruesome pictures."

Sarah looked up at her brother-in-law. "But he is my son. What can I do?"

"And he is a Fawcett and he isn't even eighteen. We will help him. We will go to see Jeremiah Botsford tomorrow. I will make an appointment." Standing up he smiled, "Now let's go tickle that grandson of yours."

The next day, Sarah and John entered the offices of Jeremiah Botsford at the agreed upon time and sat down in the plush, green leather chairs while Judge Botsford sat behind a desk that was mounded with stacks of papers. Sarah mused to herself that if a person started to read them all now, they probably wouldn't finish in a lifetime.

"John. Nice to see you again." Botsford shook his hand warmly. "I understand that you are still writing and stirring up problems for us politicians. Doesn't that family of grandchildren keep you busy enough? How's Emily?"

John marveled that an important man like Jeremiah Botsford could keep everybody straight. He seemed to have a gift for names.

"Sarah." He slowed his speech and lowered his voice and holding her hand in both of his, he said, "We were really sorry to hear about William. He was a wonderful human being and universally loved. How's Elizabeth? And how's Rufus handling it?"

John took over. "That is what we are here about, Judge. As you know, Rufus is to be tried for murder when the court meets in September. Frankly, we don't know what to do. We thought maybe you could help."

Botsford removed his spectacles and threw them amidst the sea of papers. "I see," he said rising and walking over to the open door of his office. He called through the open door to whomever might be in earshot, "I'm not to be disturbed." Then to emphasize the point he swung the door shut with a bang. Turning to his two guests, he said, "First I want you to tell me all about it."

When John and Sarah had finished relating all the salient details to Judge Botsford, they sat back and waited for his response.

"You know that I am not in practice anymore. I am not even a judge. I work as the Solicitor General, which is a fancy way of saying that I defend the government from the results of their own stupidity." He chuckled at his own joke then seemed to realize that neither John nor Sarah were smiling.

"Hmmm, yes," he continued. He began shuffling through some papers and grabbed one with some amazement as well as with obvious pleasure that he was able to find what he wanted. "Andrew Bliss will be the judge assigned to the case and I would not talk to him. I could not interfere, even if it would do any good. You are better to opt for a jury trial which is your right. In a case like this, a murder case, it is more advantageous to have it decided by a jury, twelve men from the community. Don't let anybody tell you any differently."

Botsford continued rummaging through his papers, intent on finding something else. "Bliss is a good man, a good judge. He has a relaxed manner, not stuffy, but he runs a tight court. There'll be no shenanigans going on with him in charge. Young Rufus will get a fair trial. But we still want to throw him on the mercy of your friends and neighbours, not just some crusty old judge who will merely interpret the law."

Sarah noticed how the Judge had switched to the use of "we" instead of "you" in discussing the strategy. She liked this change. It gave her some hope.

He looked up at John and Sarah as if challenging either one of them to disagree with what he had said. "Timothy Shannon will likely act for the Crown. He's been doing a lot of that sort of thing lately. I've had my run-ins with Shannon and I don't particularly like him much. He's an unimaginative little man but he seems to be making a name for himself. He'll dot the I's and cross the T's. There's nothing we can do about that."

The Judge stopped and looking sheepishly at John and Sarah, he asked, "Would you like a cup of coffee or tea?" They both shook their heads.

"You know, an increasing number of people are choosing to use a lawyer to defend them in court. Instead of speaking for themselves they hire one of us. It'll cost you money but from what you say about Rufus, it might be a good idea. Sometimes it helps."

John reassured him, "The money isn't a problem."

"Good. Now let's see. Chandler and Stewart are getting a lot of action and they're good. Thomas Chandler is a busy man but I probably could get him to handle it. Did Charles Chandler investigate?"

John and Sarah both nodded.

"In that case, I wouldn't advise either him or Stewart." He leaned over as if to let them in on a secret. "Chandler's his cousin. In some instances it might work for us but not in this one. Sheriff Chandler's reputation will be riding on this and you know how family is." Botsford regretted saying this last statement as soon as it left his mouth.

"Ahh, here they are." Botsford rescued his spectacles from under a brief. "I'm always losing these damn things. Now where were we?" He thought for a minute. "You know I might have just the man. About five years ago I had a young fellow come work for me, Edward Morse. He studied down in Massachusetts. He's been studying here, too, has done some

ROBERT JAMES

things for me. If the truth be known, the fact that I have this job is largely due to him."

He paused in thought for a minute and then he removed his spectacles and threw them back down under some papers. "Yes, he's just the man. He's capable. Be good for him, too." Without waiting for a response, Botsford opened the door wide and screamed, "Edward. Ed. Get in here." Then he added as an afterthought to whomever was listening, "I don't want to be disturbed."

Turning back to Sarah and John, he looked very serious. "I won't fool you. It does not look good. If Edward can save Rufus from the gallows, that alone might be considered a victory."

So it was decided. Edward Morse would represent Rufus Fawcett in the matter of the Crown versus Rufus Fawcett, charged with the murder of his father, William Fawcett, on or about June 19, 1832, in the town of Sackville, New Brunswick. His first official act on behalf of the family was to present bail for Rufus.

Morse arrived at the jail the next day. As he looked over the small building, he gave a shudder. Rufus was in a small cell, dark and damp with no means of washing and no ventilation, with hardly enough room to lie down. Fortunate that it was summer as there had been little thought given to providing heat, he had only one blanket and the clothes on his back; the bed was a pile of straw in one corner.

Morse could not believe the overpowering stench which greeted him.

Addressing the jailer, he said, "That's awful. No man should be forced to live in a smell like that. I have a good mind to report you."

Picking his teeth with a piece of straw, the man looked contemptuously at Morse. "You must be new at this. I fumigate all of them every day with vinegar just like I'm supposed to.

He should be thankful. The whole place was white-washed last month; it keeps down the lice."

Rufus was fortunate that he had a cell to himself as there were no separate women's facilities and often children as young as eight were incarcerated. In busy times he would have been manacled or chained and forced to share this cubicle.

The jailer was given a set amount of money to run this operation and from this money he had to buy supplies and pay himself. The requirement was that daily he provide a pound and a half of bread plus water to each prisoner. In some establishments the inmates had to grind their own wheat, but he was very proud of the fact that he bought the bread from a local woman who made certain that each loaf was the prescribed weight. He wasn't like some jailers who skimped to augment a meager salary.

"Look. I passed on the extra food that his mother sent over every day. Didn't have to. That's the thanks I get." He did not add that he did keep a little of Sarah's cooking for himself and, of course, she had been astute enough to include some for him as well. Shaking his head he added, "Good luck with that one. He's a queer duck. Never seen one like him before. He doesn't say two words, just as cool as you please — so young, too."

Although Rufus was grateful to be released after two days in jail, he was miffed that it had been to the custody of his Uncle Johnnie under who's roof he would be forced to live until the trial. As Morse undertook to deliver him to that house, he quickly gained the typical impressions of Rufus and on that short buggy ride, he vowed that there would be absolutely no way he would ever let this young man testify in his own defense.

James and Elizabeth were quite pleased that Rufus was at Uncle John's as they were able to carry on as normal a life as possible for the rest of the summer. They seldom visited him inasmuch as Elizabeth was busy with Willie and James was totally involved in the farm. Even had he wanted to, he did not have any spare time or energy to devote to his young brother-in-law.

"Will has agreed to help with the farming so that will be a great help. I believe that it may be because he wants to get away from the house, with Rufus there."

Edward Morse met with John, Sarah, James and Elizabeth on August 26, just three days after Will's marriage to Martha Chappell. With the trial set to commence on September 4, he wanted to take the opportunity to review his case.

"On the positive side, it is in our favour that this trial will proceed before Rufus turns eighteen on September 14. I would prefer to be defending a seventeen-year-old than a man eighteen years of age. I do not want to deceive you," he said solemnly. "Things do not look good. I know their case and it is compelling. If you have any influence with young Rufus you might persuade him to change his demeanor. The jury will be watching him, examining him to see how he reacts to every word, to every nuance in the courtroom. I sometimes believe that he doesn't understand what is at stake here."

Sarah, brightening, asked, "So you think his being seventeen might cause the jury to be lenient with him? Even if he's found guilty, perhaps they will choose a lesser penalty?"

Morse looked at her in shock. "Mrs. Fawcett, the jury does not decide the sentence. I thought that you understood that. I am sorry if I have misled you in any way. Guilt or innocence, alone, is decided by the jury. Then their job is done. The sentence is decided by the magistrate. The judge decides the fate of the accused."

It was obvious that none of them at the table had realized that fact. The news was not good.

Sarah asked tentatively, "And if he is found guilty, what is that fate likely to be?"

They all stared at Edward Morse. He rubbed the palm of his hand thoughtfully across the table. "I do not think that it would accomplish anything at this juncture to speculate. Let's leave that until we know what direction the trial is going."

Although Edward Morse did not venture an opinion, neither John nor James nor Elizabeth nor Sarah had any doubt what the sentence would be.

Chapter XIX

September 4 was a rainy day in Sackville. The temperature was both a reminder that the summer was ending and a preview that the worst was yet to come. It did not diminish the crowd that pushed and shoved their way inside the new courthouse to get a seat for the proceedings. Content to sit on the backless benches, they dressed up for the occasion and some had even packed a lunch so that they could make a day of it.

When asked why they were there, many would say that it was to offer support to the Fawcetts who were their neighbours or their friends. Others would take a moral position and answer that they were there to see justice done; either to see an innocent young man set free or a murderer receive his due. In truth, most who attended did so because it was a great show, great entertainment. This trial was the most exciting event that most of them could remember. The rumours, the facts surrounding it made it even more alluring. That it involved a prominent Sackville family, both as the victim and as the alleged perpetrator, raised this case to irresistible.

Sackville had very little crime. Theft was extremely rare, because of the harsh penalties associated with it. Being branded in the hand with a searing hot coin was enough to make the petty thieves stop and reconsider. Furthermore, this community was made up of mostly farmers, honest and unsophisticated, who behaved the law because it was the right thing to do. "It's not like Saint John" was a common phrase used to describe their neighborhood.

Judge Andrew Bliss was seated behind the desk when the doors opened for spectators. The front of his desk was paneled so that no one could see behind. As well, it was on a raised platform backing to the door leading to the judge's chambers. The reason for this elaborate arrangement was his gout. His massive size and fondness for clarets and rich food had resulted in bandaged feet that he attempted to hide from the public. By being previously seated he could avoid an obvious entrance and, when he did need to leave, he could simply turn around and duck out the door.

The twelve jurors had been selected and were receiving their instructions. Josiah Hicks was appointed foreman and was ready to lead them in to the corralled area that would set them apart as having an important and serious duty. Not one of them would have dreamed of being excused from this privilege, as it was an honour to be serving on this jury. They took their responsibility seriously.

Before the prisoner was led out, Judge Bliss called the two attorneys to the bench. "Good morning gentlemen. I trust that both of you know how I like to run my court." Stifling a belch, he looked at Timothy Shannon. "Now Tim, you know by now what I will and will not allow. You, Mr. Morse, I am sure that Jeremiah has coached you plenty." His eyes were twinkling. "Now if you hear me cough, that's your signal to ask for a recess, 'cause I got to go. Agreed?"

"Agreed, Your Honour," they both recited.

"Both ready?" he asked.

"Ready, Your Honour," they both intoned.

"Witnesses all here?"

"All here, Your Honour," they agreed.

"Now I have a full docket and I'd like to move this thing along. No opening arguments, ten minutes each for closings. I figure three days tops for the whole thing. This is not a tough case. Any problems with that?"

"None, Your Honour." Each looked at the other.

"Now any questions before I ask for the prisoner and the jury to be brought out?"

"No," said Shannon and turned to leave.

"Just one, your honour," answered Morse.

Shannon stopped dead in his tracks and turned slowly around. What could this young lawyer possibly want to ask? Bliss would kill him.

In a most apologetic tone, Morse asked, "I would like to have the accused sit with me at the defense table rather than sit in the prisoner's dock."

"Reasons?" asked Bliss.

"Well, some enlightened jurists believe that it prevents juries from making up their minds before they hear any evidence. It also gives me a chance to confer with the accused and, finally, it is simply more humane."

The Judge turned to Shannon, "Problems with that?"

"Problems? I should say so," he replied indignantly. He knew Bliss was going to crucify this new lawyer any minute. "Why, what if he escapes or something. I have never heard of such an outrageous thing. Your Honour, it is asinine."

"Oh, Tim. I think we'll take a chance on this one. Permission granted." The Judge smiled. "'Enlightened jurists,' eh? I see you've read my paper on 'The Humane Treatment of Prisoners'."

Morse smiled back. He had won this round and given Shannon something to think about. However there was going to have to be a lot more victories to win this battle.

As James George sat in the gallery and watched the two lawyers he felt that Timothy Shannon was definitely a dandy. He did not wear his clothes, he displayed them. His hands were constantly busy removing a speck of dirt from his sleeve, smoothing his hair, straightening his waistcoat. While projecting an arrogant attitude that dared anyone to differ with him, his reputation was one of a hard-hitting prosecutor who could be classified as relentless. Later, James described him to Elizabeth as the only man he knew who could strut while sitting down.

The accused was led out and sat with Edward Morse at the defense table. Rufus was dressed as Morse had indicated although he did look around and wave at some of his friends in the gallery. He looked quite relaxed as if he was unbothered by the whole thing.

The jury took their places. Morse had learned not to try to judge a jury by their looks. He had been fooled many times before and he believed that it was best to ignore any concerns or preconceived notions about the twelve men.

James liked Edward Morse for he had a genuine smile and was not afraid to use it. Unlike a lot of his peers, Edward was a good listener and not at all patronizing. He had a habit of cocking his head to one side and nodding in agreement when someone else was talking. The two men enjoyed each other's company and had sought each other's opinions in the days before the trial.

The first witness for the prosecution was Doctor Smith. Morse was happy to have his testimony first as he did not want the gory details to be the last thing on the jury's mind. Smith described the wound and the cause of death and identified the slug that had been pried from William's chest. His testimony was straight forward and he had obviously testified before as he did so without unnecessary inflection or emotion. Morse felt that the quicker they left this line of testimony, the better for his client. At this point Shannon started an interesting line of testimony.

Shannon: (Holding up the slug) "Doctor, this is the slug that killed William Fawcett."
Smith: "Yes. That is the one."
Shannon: (Handing him a live bullet) "What is this?"
Smith: "That appears to be live ammunition of the same type."
Shannon: "The same type that killed Mr. Fawcett? You can tell that, Doctor?"
Smith: "Each bullet or slug has identifying characteristics and you can see here," (Pointing to the two exhibits) "these are the same."
Shannon: "Amazing, Doctor. What about this?" (Handing him a spent casing).
Smith: "Why, that is the same as well. This is a brass that would hold such a slug."
Chandler: "Thank you, Doctor. Your witness."

Edward Morse walked slowly to the front. He hadn't expected this line of testimony.

Morse: "Doctor, how can you be so sure about all this? You're a medical doctor aren't you?"
Smith: "Yes. I am a medical doctor. But you see, Mr. Morse, all ammunition is unique. I make a bit of a hobby out of this. I guess I'm considered a bit of an expert and have testified in many cases. I am absolutely sure that this slug, this casing and this live piece of ammunition are all of the same type."

Dejectedly, Morse walked back to his seat. He had been unprepared for this line of questioning and Smith had told him more than he wanted to know. He knew better than that. He must be more careful in his questioning.

The next witness was Sheriff Charles Chandler. Most of his testimony was predictable, dealing with who was at the Fawcett house that night, what he had done when he got there and situation of the body. Morse was surprised to see that Chandler had some pages with him where he had written down some notes. Morse had heard of police officers doing this but it was not a very common practice. It also derailed one of his favourite tactics for he loved to try to confuse a witness or question his memory. This was going to be a very difficult case. Finally Shannon came to the part about questioning Rufus.

Shannon: "What did Rufus Fawcett say when he entered the house?"
Chandler: "He asked, "What was happening.""
Shannon: "And then?"
Chandler: "When he was told that his father had been killed he asked, 'Have the Indians killed my father?'"
Shannon: "What did you take that to mean?"
Chandler: "Well I'm not rightly sure. I didn't know what he meant."

There was laughter from the spectators but Judge Bliss quickly brought that to an end.

Shannon: "Was that a usual thing to say? Were there Indians in the area that were killing people, threatening people, harming people?"
Chandler: "Not that I know of? No, we haven't had problems with Indians here for a long time."
Shannon: "So he was making it up. It was an excuse then?"

"Objection." Now this was the moment that Morse wanted, his first opportunity to address the jury directly. He got to his feet and looking at each jury member in turn, he said in a southern drawl, "Now I'm sure that Mr. Shannon would like to have all these men believe that the defendant was making up an excuse but they're much too smart for that." He stopped and smiled. "They know that there is no possible way that Sheriff Chandler, great lawman though he is, could enter Rufus Fawcett's mind and know why he said that." There was a twitter of chuckles.

"Mr. Morse. I will sustain your objection." The judge was not smiling. "However, no more speeches. And drop the southern drawl. I'm from the north." This time there was real laughter. The judge had just spanked Morse for all to see.

"Continue, Mr. Shannon."

Shannon: "Describe Rufus Fawcett's reactions when he saw his murdered father."

Chandler: "He was very calm, very cool, not excited or upset."

Shannon: "From what you have seen before, is that normal?"

Chandler: "No, not at all. Usually the relative of a murdered person would be really angry or disturbed."

Shannon: "Now describe what happened when you asked him where he had been?"

Chandler: (Checking his notes before he began) "Well, he was kind of mixed up. First, he said he was at the house all the time. Then he said that he went for a walk. Then he said that he was out with some friends, but he couldn't remember their names. Then he said he was at the tavern. Finally he remembered that he went down to the marsh to get the cattle."

Shannon: "As an experienced sheriff, is that normal, not knowing where you've been?"

Chandler: "Well, no, but it does happen, when a person is shocked by something and is confused."

Shannon: "Now, Sheriff, which one of these, ah, one, two, three, four, five, yes, five, ah, stories did he stick to?"

Chandler: "Well, he said that he left the Fawcett farm at eight o'clock and went down to the marsh and chased the cows and arrived home about ten-thirty."

Shannon: "How long does it take to get to the marsh?"

Chandler: "Well, a good hour there in the dark, I suppose."

Shannon: "And a good hour back?"

Chandler: "Uh-huh."

Shannon: "Ten-thirty. Half an hour after the murder. So if he was in the marsh he couldn't have shot his father through the kitchen window and killed him. Right?"

Chandler: "Well, no. I guess that's right."

Shannon: "So if somebody saw him in the marsh that would be a pretty good alibi."

Chandler: "It certainly would."

Shannon: "Or if someone saw him around his house at say eight-thirty or nine-thirty, that would be pretty damaging to the accused."

Chandler: "I suppose so."

Judge Bliss was getting a little antsy. "Is this going somewhere, Mr. Shannon?"

Timothy Shannon smiled, "I'll leave this line of questioning for now." He scratched his head, "I'm just a mite confused."

Edward Morse would have bet that he wasn't in the least bit confused. In fact, he had probably never been confused a day in his life.

Shannon: "Now, was a murder weapon found?"

Chandler: "Yes, George Lawrence found a rifle in the garden, over the fence."

Shannon: (Handing him a gun) "In the garden? Is this the gun?"

Chandler: "Yes, I'd say so."

Shannon: "Did you show this rifle to Rufus Fawcett?"

Chandler: "Well, yes, but he said he had never seen it before."

Shannon: "Never seen it before. Is he familiar with guns?"

Chandler: "He told me the night of the murder that he hadn't fired a gun in a long time, maybe a couple of months before."

Shannon: "I see. So that would make it about the middle of April that he had last fired a gun. Didn't he like hunting? All boys like hunting."

Chandler: "He told me, no, that he hated hunting."

Shannon: "Getting back to this rifle for a minute, what kind of ammunition does it shoot?"

Chandler: "The same kind that Dr. Smith was looking at."

Shannon: (Pointing to the exhibits) "This gun shoots this kind of ammunition?"

Chandler: "Yes."

Shannon: "The same as the slug that was in William Fawcett and the same as this casing?"

Chandler: "The very same."

Shannon: "By the way, Sheriff, where did this spent casing come from?"

Chandler: "If it is the one I gave you, I ejected it from that rifle there that George Lawrence found."

Shannon: "Well then, I'd say we have the murder weapon, wouldn't you?"

Chandler nodded. In fact Shannon had led them through this so carefully that all the jury nodded, the spectators nodded, even Judge Bliss nodded.

Shannon: "We have the murder weapon. If we only knew who owned it. Did you have an opportunity to see where William Fawcett keeps his guns?"

Chandler: "Yes, James George opened the chest for me with a key."

Shannon: "So this chest was kept locked."

Chandler: "Yes and the key was hidden where only the family knew."

This statement brought an audible gasp from the gallery. Judge Bliss had to rap his gavel.

Shannon: "Tell us what you saw when you opened that case."

Chandler: "Well there was space for three rifles, like holders you know, but there was only two guns in the case. And there was cleaning supplies and ammunition. It was the same type of ammunition that you and Dr. Smith were looking at."

A murmur spread through the crowd. Bliss gaveled it silent.

Shannon: "The very same type of slugs and casings?"

Chandler: "You see, William was kind of particular. He kept all his shells in a bored-out case with a hole for each shell. The idea is for all the holes to be filled up with either live ammunition or spent casing jackets. That way you know if there has been any left about."

Shannon: "And all the holes were filled?"

Chandler: "Actually no. There were three empty spots."

Shannon: "Hmmmm. Did you happen to ask anybody else in the Fawcett house how many rifles they had."

Chandler: "Sort of. James George indicated that there were three rifles and he was very surprised when there

were only two in the case."
Shannon: "Did you ask Rufus Fawcett about this ammunition? Did he recognize it?"
Chandler: "Not at first, but later he did."
Shannon: "So at first he said he had never seen it before and then he finally admitted it was his father's?"
Chandler: "Yes, I guess so."
Shannon: "When he knew that you were on to him? When he knew you had him? When he knew that there was no way out?"

Edward Morse jumped to his feet. "Objection."
The Judge smiled. "You know better, Mr. Shannon. Though, I guess it is kind of irresistible."
Those in the audience who were not absolutely flabbergasted, laughed.

Shannon: "We're almost finished Sheriff. Tell us about the footprints."
Chandler: "Thomas Ayer found a set of footprints leading up to the kitchen window and leading back away from the kitchen window. I measured Rufus's boot in them and they were the same size."
Shannon: "Same size. Thank you. Your witness."

The Judge interrupted. "I think this would be a great time for a lunch break. We will convene at two." He turned to the two lawyers, "If you two gentlemen would please join me at the Widow Evans's place. You can split the bill."
Morse didn't feel much like lunch but he knew better than to disobey the judge. Mrs. Evans expected them and when they arrived the table was laden with meat pies and pasties and a roast of lamb with mint sauce and little red potatoes and turnips and carrots and a fresh lettuce salad. For dessert she set forth a huge bowl of trifle and they helped themselves.

Strong red wine accompanied the meal followed with glasses of port. Morse wondered if there were a Widow Evans in each town that Judge Bliss visited. No wonder he was such a size and experiencing health problems.

They talked about everything, all types of law, where they had been trained, cases they had seen, other lawyers, the state of the government in New Brunswick, everything except these particular proceedings. Edward Morse was reminded that this was a job, a game, for whatever happened in the courtroom stayed in the courtroom. At the moment they were just two attorneys and a judge enjoying lunch.

When they returned to the courthouse, Morse wondered if once more he had been the victim of a slick legal team for he was full and bloated with more need for a nap than an afternoon of cross examining witnesses. He speculated that maybe the jury was of the same mind.

Stopping to speak to James, he tried to smile and to downplay the events of the morning. "Thus far we have heard nothing new. Now it is our turn to ask the questions. Frankly I was surprised by a number of loose ends in their case and I'll attack these this afternoon."

As the court was brought to order, Edward Morse rose from the table and, shuffling through a sheaf of pages, he approached Charles Chandler, who was already in the witness stand.

Morse: "Good afternoon, Mr. Chandler. I won't take up a lot of your valuable time. I would like to clarify a few details. When you were talking about Rufus, and mentioned his asking about the Indians killing his father, you said that what he said was unusual and that his reactions were" (Checking his notes) "not normal."

Chandler: "That's correct."

Morse: "Sheriff, have you ever noticed that a person who is dazed or under shock from some terrible thing happening seems to be unusual or not normal?"

Chandler: (Scratching his head) "No, I can't say that I have, but I have noticed that murderers and the like behave very peculiar when they are trying to cover things up."

Morse: "Well, let's go on. You mentioned in your testimony that confusion and bewilderment or not knowing where you are happens when a person is shocked by something."

Chandler: "Yes, that is correct."

Morse: "As was demonstrated by Rufus Fawcett?"

Chandler: "No."

Morse: (Whirling around) "What?"

Chandler: "No, he was completely in control of himself, calm and cool, almost calculating. Yes that's it, calculating, like a cold-blooded killer. He knew what he was doing. He was simply trying to cover up where he had been and what he had done, murdering that poor man."

Morse looked up in anguish at the judge. "It was your question, Mr. Morse," replied the judge with little sympathy on his face.

They had set the trap and he had fallen into it. The bait had been laid in the earlier testimony and they had been positive that he would follow it up in his questioning and he had. They had let him ask the question that would incriminate Rufus.

Morse: (Scrambling to get back on track) "But you did say that if he was down at the marsh, he couldn't commit the murder."

Chandler: "I did say that. If Rufus Fawcett left for the marsh at eight o'clock and rode down there and chased up the animals and rode back, I don't see how he could be back in time to murder his father. Yes, that's true."

Morse: "Now this rifle that was found in the garden, it could have been dropped there a week before, couldn't it?"

Chandler: "I don't see how. You see, I smelled it and it had been fired recently, I'd say within the hour, and there was a residue of gun powder in the barrel and on the breach. I got it all over my hands."

Morse had been trapped again. They were deliberately setting him up to ask the key questions and he was falling for it like the rookie he was.

Morse: (Exasperated) "But, Sheriff, isn't it true that you don't know that this was William Fawcett's rifle?"

Chandler: "Yes, sir, that's true."

Morse felt he had salvaged a little. Still it had been a difficult afternoon. He had been taught some lessons.

Morse: "And the footprints, aren't there a lot of people who wear the size boots that would fit into those prints?"

Chandler: "Well, not me." (Everybody laughs) "But, yes, I suppose you are right. They were an average size, not particularly big and not particularly small."

Morse: "So the fact that Rufus Fawcett's boot fit into those footprints outside the kitchen window, was not all that remarkable."

Chandler: "I suppose you are right. The size, alone, wasn't all that remarkable."

Morse stopped. He didn't know what the Sheriff meant by "the size, alone," and he certainly wasn't going to ask. He felt that before too long it would be revealed to him. He turned to the judge, "No more questions."

Judge Bliss said, "I think this is a good place to end today. We'll pick this up again tomorrow."

So the first day of testimony was over and Edward Morse felt exhausted. His shirt was sticking to his back, his hands were clammy and he was livid. When he met with Rufus the exasperation showed all over his face. "I told you to tell me everything. I told you that if I was going to defend you, I needed to be aware of every little detail. Are there any more surprises for that lawyer to spring on me tomorrow? I need to know."

Rufus was as calm and as sure as ever. "You're doing fine Mr. Morse. Don't worry."

Chapter XX

The next day, September 5, the weather was even worse as the rain was pouring down and the temperature colder. The crowds were larger and Edward Morse figured that the news of yesterday's massacre in the courtroom must have been passed from neighbour to neighbour with the result that more wanted to be present for the action today.

As he walked up the front steps of the courthouse he sensed a different welcome from the people milling about outside. Yesterday he had been a bit of a novelty, a celebrity whom the residents wanted to meet and talk to. They had asked him, "How do you think it's going to go?" or "Do you think that Rufus did it?" or wished him, "Good luck." Today they shunned him as if he were the carrier of some abomination that, by mere association, might infect them. He did not mind their avoiding him but he wasn't fond of their reason for doing so.

Judge Bliss smiled and he was not sure if it was a smile of welcome or one of pity. The jury, when seated turned their

eyes to the judge or to the gallery or to the prosecution table —
anywhere but in his direction.

Edward Morse looked over to Rufus. Rufus turned to him
and asked, "How are you holding up?" It should have been
he who asked Rufus that question.

Timothy Shannon wore a bright coloured waistcoat. His
hair was slicked down and he had a wide smile on his face.
Obviously, he was feeling quite chipper this morning. He did
not even glance in their direction.

Shannon: "The Crown calls Thomas Weaton."

Weaton identified himself as a neighbour of the Fawcetts
and placed himself at home on the night of June 19.

Shannon: "Would you tell us what happened before you
heard the alarm?"
Weaton: "I was coming in from the barn when I saw young
Rufus down by the fence that runs along the road."
Shannon: "What time was this?"
Weaton: "It was about eight-thirty. I had finished the
milking and saw somebody kind of crouched
behind the fence, so I went down. I guess I must
have scared him."
Shannon: "Why do you say that?"
Weaton: "Well, he jumped when I spoke to him."
Shannon: "How did you know that it was Rufus Fawcett?"
Weaton: "Well, I have knowed him since he was a baby
carried around by his mother. I guess I know Rufus
Fawcett all right. Besides I spoke to him."
Shannon: "What did you say?"
Weaton: "Why I said, 'Is that you Rufus?'"
Shannon: "And what did he say?"
Weaton: "Well, he said, 'Yup'."

There was a titter through the crowd but the seriousness of what was said far outweighed the humour of the way it was presented.

Shannon: "No more questions."

Edward Morse took a deep breath and waded in.

Morse: "Could you have been wrong about the time? You were working in the barn, it is difficult to judge time exactly. Could you have been wrong about it being eight-thirty?"

Weaton: "Well, I guess I could be, a little. Yes, that's possible. It might have been closer to nine o'clock. Yes, it was probably closer to nine o'clock."

Morse felt sick. This was not at all the direction that he had been hoping to go. This case was going from bad to worse. Nine o'clock was worse than eight-thirty. It seemed every time that he questioned a witness the result was disastrous.

Morse: "No more questions."

Morse sat down wondering what else could possibly happen.

As if to respond to his thoughts, Shannon spoke.

Shannon: "The Crown calls Tolar Thompson."

After establishing the usual background, Shannon dropped the bombshell.

Shannon: "Did anything unusual happen that evening before you heard the alarm?"

Thompson: "At about nine-thirty, I saw Rufus Fawcett hiding
        in the abandoned well at my place."
Shannon: "Hiding?"
Thompson: "Yes, sir. He was stooped down, peaking out from
        inside the well."

Morse gritted his teeth and stared at Rufus. Rufus grinned
back. He caught the eye of one of his pals in the audience and
winked.

Shannon: "Did you ask him what he was doing?"
Thompson: "Yes, and he told me that he was hiding from his
        friends."
Shannon: "Did that seem unusual to you?"
Thompson: "Well, yes, until I heard what happened to William.
        Then, of course, I knew."

Morse decided to let this slip go. He was getting reluctant
to stir up the hornet's nest.

Shannon: "You know the area well, Mr. Thompson. If Rufus
        Fawcett was seen in your well at nine-thirty, and
        at Weaton's fence at eight-thirty or nine, could he
        possibly ride to the marsh and back by ten-thirty?"
Thompson: "I don't think so."
Shannon: "I don't think so either, Mr. Thompson. I don't
        think that even Mark Campbell delivering the mail
        on that fast horse of his in broad daylight at a full
        gallop on a good day could make it in that time.
        Of course he'd be stopping here and there to wet
        his whistle."

The crowd roared.
It took five raps of Bliss's gavel and a threat of clearing
the courtroom to quiet the spectators. The jurors were having

trouble stifling their laughs, all except the foreman, Josiah Hicks. Timothy Shannon was severely chastised but, as any trial lawyer would say, it was worth it.

Again it was the defense's turn to question.

Morse: "Is it possible that on that dark night from a distance that you might have been mistaken about the identity of the person hiding in the well? Could it have been a tramp, a passer-by, perhaps a peddler?"

Thompson: "Well it is possible I suppose...."

Morse: (Cutting him off) "Thank you. That's all."

Shannon didn't bother to challenge. No one in that courtroom believed that Tolar Thompson was mistaken, not Thompson, not the Judge, not the jury, and not Morse.

The next three witnesses were neighbours who positively identified the rifle as one belonging to William Fawcett. William had purchased it from one of them and the other two had hunted with the deceased several times and knew his guns. Shannon made valuable points on the fact that Rufus had denied knowing that the gun was his father's, asking each witness if he could think of any reason why Rufus would not be able to identify it.

Morse was able to invoke limited damage control by playing on Rufus's possible confusion that night. He tried to convince them that the shock of the situation had caused bewilderment in the young lad. He was moderately successful, until Shannon called on Joseph and Frederick Sears, the Fawcett's next door neighbours.

The first to testify was the son, Frederick. Frederick admitted to knowing Rufus, and chumming around with him for some time.

Shannon: "Does Rufus like to hunt?"

Sears: "Not really. He used to go out with us occasionally but I haven't seen him hunt for a year or two. He didn't really like it too much."

Shannon: "So if Rufus Fawcett said he hadn't hunted with a gun for a couple of months, since the middle of April, he would be correct?"

Sears: "Yes, sir, I haven't seen him hunting for a long time."

Shannon: "But Rufus didn't say that, did he? He said that he hadn't fired a gun for a couple of months, didn't he? Have you seen him fire a gun since the middle of April?"

Sears: "Well, I guess I have."

Shannon: "Have you or not?"

Sears: "Yes, I have."

Shannon: "How many times?"

Sears: "I guess maybe five or ten."

Shannon: "Five or ten? Now, Mr. Sears, there is a lot of difference between five and ten. Now which is it? Closer to five or closer to ten?"

Sears: "Well, I guess, ten."

Shannon: "When was the last time you saw him fire a gun?"

Sears: "Probably a couple of days before Mr. Fawcett was shot."

Shannon: "How many times between June 1 and June 19?"

Sears: "Maybe five."

Shannon: (Going in for the kill) "Now, if he wasn't hunting, but he was firing a gun, what was he doing?"

Sears: "He was target practicing."

Shannon: "Target practicing. That seems like a stupid thing for anyone to do. Why would anyone practice shooting at targets?"

Sears: (Trying to defend one of his favourite pastimes) "Why, no, sir. You target practice to get better, to improve your aim. Everybody practices."

Shannon: "To make sure you hit where you're aiming? To kill what you're aiming at?"

Sears: "Yes, sir."

Shannon: "What was Rufus meaning to kill? If he didn't like hunting, what or whom was he practicing killing? What game was he after?"

Morse blasted to his feet sending papers flying. "I object, Your Honour."

Shannon withdrew the question, but they all heard the question and they all knew the answer. The damage had been done. Timothy Shannon had led them along, through his questions to Frederick Sears, to the logical conclusion.

Joseph Sears, Frederick's father, gave essentially the same testimony. Morse recovered a bit since he was able to get them to admit that some people shoot guns for fun and do target practice for fun. But, everybody knew that Rufus didn't appear to be one of those people.

After a short recess, Shannon introduced his key witness. True to his form, he had kept this one secret.

Shannon: "The Crown calls on John W. Dixon."

As Dixon became settled in the witness box, Timothy Shannon approached him very slowly. He was enjoying this as a cat enjoys stalking a mouse.

Shannon: "Mr. Dixon, what do you do?"

Dixon: "I am a bootmaker."

Shannon: "You only make boots?"

Dixon: "No, I make men's boots and men's shoes. I do a limited amount of other leather work, bridles and suchlike."

Shannon: "Have you ever been to the Fawcett farm?"

Dixon: "Yes, on one occasion."

Shannon: "Tell us about that."

Dixon: "Sheriff Chandler took me out to the Fawcett place on June 20, to look at some footprints outside the kitchen window."

Shannon: "Now, these were footprints that he believed were made by the murderer who shot William Fawcett?"

Dixon: "Yes. That is correct."

Shannon: "Did you compare Rufus Fawcett's boots to these footprints?"

Dixon: "Yes. We did and they fit exactly."

Shannon: "But Rufus's size is a common size, is it not?"

Dixon: "Fairly common. Probably about one in five pairs of the boots I make are close to that size."

Shannon: "Did you notice anything peculiar about these footprints?"

Dixon: "Yes. I made the boots that created these prints. You see, I put a special mark in the sole of my boots which identifies me as the bootmaker. Like this." (He showed the sole of a new pair of boots.)

Shannon took a long time walking around the courtroom showing this pair of boots to the judge, the jury, the defense table and most of the front row of the gallery. This was his finest hour and he was going to enjoy every minute of it.

Shannon: "And Rufus's boots had your mark on their sole?"

Dixon: "Yes, Sir. There is no doubt about it. I made the boots that made those footprints and I made Rufus Fawcett's boots."

Shannon: "You remember him as a customer?"

Dixon: "I sure do."

Shannon: "And Rufus Fawcett's boots fit the size and shape of the footprints that we suspect were made by the murderer?"

Dixon: "His boots fit the prints exactly."

Shannon: "And you recall Rufus Fawcett buying boots from
          you?"
Dixon: "I sure do."
Shannon: "Your witness."

Edward Morse walked quickly to Mr. John W. Dixon.

Morse: "You said that these footprints were made by boots
          of a fairly common size; so common that about
          one in five pairs that you make are this size. Is
          that correct?"
Dixon: "Yes. That's about right."
Morse: "You are a bootmaker of some renown. How many
          pairs of boots would you make in a year?"
Dixon: "It takes me about five to seven days to make a
          pair."
Morse: "Let's say, fifty a year. Is that fair?"
Dixon: "Yes, more or less."
Morse: "How many years have you been in business?"
Dixon: "Twelve, sir." (He sounds proud of his craft)
Morse: "Now, let's see. Fifty times twelve. There are
          probably six hundred pairs of your boots walking
          around New Brunswick. A lot of men buy your
          excellent boots. I trust they would last that long."
          (He emphasized "last" but no one seemed to get
          the pun.)
Dixon: "I hope so."
Morse: "So one in five means there are one hundred and
          twenty, let's be generous to the Crown and say
          one hundred pairs of your boots, of the proper size,
          with this mark, that could make those footprints?"

Morse stopped and felt faint. As soon as he said it, he
knew that once again, Timothy Shannon had suckered him
into asking the very question that they wanted asked. He played

on Morse's vanity as a young, confident lawyer. The facts were too obvious. No Crown Attorney would leave himself open like that unless he were a fool and Timothy Shannon was no fool.

Dixon: "Not exactly, sir." (Looking surprised.) "You see, I only made one pair of boots with the particular mark in the sole that made the footprints at William Fawcett's..."

The courtroom was completely silent. No one moved. Every person in the room was holding his breath and yet every person knew what Mr. John W. Dixon, bootmaker, was going to say next.

Dixon: "...and that pair was special for Rufus Fawcett."

The gallery exploded. No amount of smashes by Bliss's gavel could restore order. It took five minutes and several threats of banishment and even jail to settle them down.

Weakly, Morse tried to continue. He tried to elicit the fact that Rufus's footprints around the house were a perfectly normal thing and in no way meant that he had committed the crime but Morse's heart wasn't in it. The jury weren't even listening, except for Rufus and Josiah Hicks who were both as impassive as ever.

Morse had committed the unforgivable sin for a trial lawyer. He had asked a witness whom he didn't know, whom he hadn't met, whom he hadn't prepped, a question for which he didn't know the answer. Never ask a question, unless you know the answer. His professors had drummed that into his head innumerable times, yet he had done just that.

Timothy Shannon had presented evidence that put Rufus at the scene of the crime. As well, he had put forth a strong string of circumstantial evidence, most of it Rufus's own doing, which seemed to incriminate Rufus. All that was left was to provide motive, the why of the event.

The three witnesses to testify to establish motive were regulars at the tavern. They were not an impressive lot, in fact they were by no means the backbone of the Sackville community but, they were Rufus's drinking buddies and the closest thing to friends that he had. Alike in their testimony in most respects, that of Nelson Bulmer was representative.

Shannon: "Good morning, Mr. Bulmer"
Bulmer: "My friends call me 'Nels.'"
Shannon: "All right, Nels..."
Bulmer: "I said, 'My friends call me 'Nels.' You can call me 'Mr. Bulmer'.""

Bulmer's friends hooted at this. This was their type of humour and finally someone was putting this big shot lawyer in his place. Shannon tried again.

Shannon: "Do you know the defendant, Rufus Fawcett?"
Bulmer: "Certainly, I know Rufus. He is a good buddy of mine. He's a good friend."
Shannon: "Do you recall an occasion, a few days prior to William Fawcett's murder, when Rufus was in the tavern?"
Bulmer: "There were many occasions when Rufus was in the tavern."
Shannon: "Yes, well on this occasion, he made an announcement about the disposal of the farm."
Bulmer: "I sure do. He and his sister were going to split the ownership of the farm."
Shannon: "Do you recall what he said?"
Bulmer: "Yes, I do. He said that there was going to be a big overturn in the house of his father."

Shannon: "He said that? You mean to say that just prior to his father's murder, Rufus announced that there were going to be big changes at the Fawcett farm?"

Bulmer: "Yes, sir."

Shannon: "Do you think he meant it?"

Bulmer: "Yes, sir. Rufus is a man of his word. I don't 'think' he meant it, I know he meant it."

Shannon: "Now, who do you think Rufus meant was going to cause this big overturn?"

Bulmer: "No question about that. He, Rufus, was going to cause the changes."

Shannon: "Now, Rufus had a girlfriend, Eliza Cornwall. Did Rufus say what his father thought about his marrying her?"

Bulmer: "Yes. He said his father got angry, that he didn't like the idea."

Shannon: "Thank you. Your witness."

Edward Morse approached Nelson Bulmer.

Morse: "Mr. Bulmer..."

Bulmer: "You can call me 'Nels,' all my friends do."

The gallery responded appreciatively and Judge Bliss did not even try to stop them.

Morse: "Nels, describe how Rufus appeared when he said those things."

Bulmer: "He was quiet, thoughtful."

Morse: "Not like a murderer who was planning his father's death?"

Bulmer: (Surprised.) "No, not at all. Like somebody who's going to change his life."

Morse: "What did you take him to mean when he announced that there was going to be a big overturn in his father's house?"

Bulmer: "That's easy. He and Eliza were going to get married and move into the Fawcett place and manage his father's affairs. That was the big overturn and all that responsibility, well, that was worrying Rufus."

Morse: "Eliza was his girlfriend?"

Bulmer: "Yes. He loved her and was going to marry her."

Morse: "But, Mr. Fawcett didn't like her."

Bulmer: "I didn't say that. I said that he didn't like the idea of Rufus marrying her. He didn't even know her 'cause he hadn't even met her. I'll tell you, when Mr. Fawcett met Eliza, he'd like her. We all do. I don't think Rufus's father would have liked the idea of him marrying any girl. He's only seventeen."

Morse: "Thank you, Nels. Thank you very much. You may step down."

Edward Morse refused the lunch invitation that day. He sat by himself and ate part of an apple before going for a walk down by the Bay. He loved to see the boats and the busy fisherman, the hawkers selling their wares, the farmers coming to town for the day. However, today none of it gave him any pleasure.

James found Edward and fell into step beside him, saying nothing.

Finally Morse broke the silence, "That was quite brutal in there this morning."

"One thing I have learned is you have play the hand life dealt you."

"God, James, with that attitude why even hire a lawyer? Just go in and throw yourself on the mercy of the court."

"You play the hand you're dealt but you damn well play it as best you can. Rufus hasn't made this easy on you, on any of us, but you are doing the best with what you have. I feel that way. We all feel that way."

"This afternoon I am supposed to present the defense case. We don't have a case. I based our whole defense on destroying the Crown's evidence however, it is I who have been destroyed. I don't mind playing the hand we have, but Rufus won't show me the cards. I should have done better."

James extended his hand. "I know you'll do your best. Drop around the house for supper tonight. Sarah wants to talk to you."

Morse presented the defense witnesses that afternoon. They could basically be described as character witnesses. He had people from the church appear and testify that Rufus had been a good person and done some good things. A former school teacher appeared and testified what an outstanding student Rufus had been. Neighbours talked about his sterling character. Morse even found some more desirable friends who vouched for him.

Shannon tried to dissolve any positive effect these witnesses might have had by getting out the message that yes, Rufus may have been all these things, but the evidence shows that he murdered his father. This was hard to refute. Morse had not presented one shed of evidence that Rufus had been anywhere other than at the murder scene. There was no evidence and no witnesses that would say any differently. He had presented no alternatives, no other possibilities.

Tomorrow they would present the closing arguments and the jury would retire to decide. Not one person in that courtroom had any doubt about what the facts suggested and what the verdict should be.

Chapter XXI

That evening of September 5, 1832, three extraordinary meetings took place in Sackville.

It was still raining when Jake Oulton walked out the door of his favourite tavern. He peered out into the darkness and turned his collar up as a protection from the cold. Casually, he sauntered around to the back of the building where a figure, dressed altogether differently, was waiting deep in the shadows. A leather bag was thrust quickly into Jake's hands.

"Jake, you are sure that you know where Josiah Hicks lives?"

"Sure, I know. I've done the odd job for him, if you get my meaning."

"You'll tell him what I said?"

"Word for word, just like you told me, I will, like I was recitin' in school." Jake coughed and spit a big wad on the ground.

"Make sure he gets all the money that's in that bag, Jake."

He wiped his mouth and nodded, "You can rely on me, you can."

The two parted. Jake returned to the tavern for a quick one to fend off the cold while the other person gave a little shiver and headed home.

In a far different part of Sackville in the faint glow of a candle, the two men had finished a delicious meal of roast venison cooked in a Cumberland sauce with yams, parsnips and fresh garden peas. With the treacle pudding but a memory, each man gazed intently into a glass of fine French cognac as they continued their conversation.

"If I do this thing, then we agree that we are even?"

"I wouldn't ask you if it weren't important. I wouldn't want to compromise you or your reputation."

"I wouldn't entertain your request if I were not obliged to you for helping me gain my position. This could cause both of us a lot of trouble."

"It is done then and we must never speak of it again."

The two judges downed the last of their drinks and went their separate ways.

In the third location, under brighter illumination, Sarah Fawcett and Edward Morse sat at the long pine table.

"Maybe I could have done better. Maybe you would have been happier with a better lawyer."

Sarah rested her hand on his. "You have done your best and I could not wish any more. You must not blame yourself. We knew that the hope was little and our chances slim. We must keep our chins up and face tomorrow as best we can."

"If only Rufus had been more cooperative. Maybe someone else could have..."

"No more. Now I need to know what will transpire tomorrow."

"The Crown will present its final arguments and I will present ours. The jury will deliberate and return a verdict. If he is found innocent, he will be free to leave, having been exonerated by the law."

"And if they find him guilty?"

"Let's not dwell on that. Let us face that..."

"I want to know," Sarah interrupted. She sat straighter in the chair and adjusted her dress. "I need to know."

"You are a remarkable woman, Mrs. Fawcett." He looked at his hands and continued reluctantly, "I am afraid that judges are not very lenient in this sort of crime. Their opinion seems to be that a trip to the gallows is a swift punishment and saves the public the cost of imprisonment."

"When? How long after?"

"Only two or three days. It avoids the chance of an appeal."

"So quickly. Who does this ghoulish duty? Who would ever agree to act as a hangman?"

"Mrs. Fawcett, I wish you wouldn't go on so with these dark questions." He gazed into her eyes but saw no lack of resolve.

Sarah returned his look and fiddled with a button on her high collar. "It is imperative that I know these things so that I can deal with them. Tell me."

"A condemned man will buy his freedom by opting for this profession as opposed to the alternative. His pay is the clothes from the executed man. The body goes for dissection."

Sarah took a deep breath. "So it is true, the story I heard, in Halifax, about pieces of a body being sold as souvenirs?"

Morse paused. "Yes. I'm sorry." He quickly added, "But I am sure that in this case, they wouldn't ...." He stopped.

Sarah shuddered; there were no tears for the time for crying had gone. Bowing her head she said a silent prayer, looked up at Morse and then said slowly, "When you give your closing argument tomorrow, remember who your audience is." She said these words very distinctly as she continued to search his eyes, looking for answers; there were none.

Edward Morse said good night and returned to his lodgings to spend yet another sleepless night. He brooded over his conversation with Sarah as he tried to organize his thoughts for his last presentation to the jury.

The rain had stopped overnight and the warm September day was a treat. Once again there were more citizens wishing entrance to the small court house than there were seats to accommodate them but that didn't stop anyone.

Sarah Fawcett, James and Elizabeth sat together, immediately behind the defense table. They wanted to be as close to Rufus as possible. Each of them knew that it might be the last time.

Morse glanced down at his rumpled pants and worn coat. It wasn't that he couldn't afford new clothes, it just seemed as if he never had the time to actually go out and buy them. He promised himself that he would remedy that after this trial was over. Staring at his counterpart with his razor creases and starched shirts, he wondered how Shannon managed to keep his clothes so neat and tidy.

As Shannon rose from his chair and walked in front of the jury, Morse noticed him pull first one shirt cuff and then the other in order to show the correct amount of sleeve below the jacket. He found this habit annoying and he had watched Shannon do this repeatedly while he stood in front of the court. It was amazing that in two short days he had become aware of the lawyer's quirks and idiosyncrasies and had grown to despise both the behavior and the man. Did the jury feel this same way? How did they feel about him?

Rufus was led in and sat down. What should he say to Rufus? What could he say, "Nice day for a hanging," or how about, "Hey Rufus, hang around after the trial"? Morse tried to dismiss these morbid thoughts from his mind for he felt badly for harbouring them but they were his way of dealing with the unthinkable.

Rufus turned to him and said, "Good morning. What day of the week is it anyway?"

Morse was amazed. It was as casual as if he were checking that the public houses were going to be open today. You never did know people.

Shannon flashed his haughty smile at the jury and began. "William Fawcett was a respected man of your community who was murdered by his son, the defendant, Rufus Fawcett. He knows that. I know that. And now, you know that.

"William Fawcett gave Rufus all the love, all the care, all the necessities that a son could possibly want. And how did he repay his father? By murdering him.

"On the evening of June 19, 1832, Rufus Fawcett ate supper with his family in the comfort of their home. His heart filled with hatred and animosity, he used a prearranged story, a falsehood, to excuse himself from the pleasures of his home. He told his parents that he was going to the marsh to find some lost animals and to cause them to return to the farm. Then he left. The facts tell you that and they don't lie.

"Having left the home, Rufus went down the lane and crouched and waited by the fence at Thomas Weaton's farm. This would have worked except Mr. Weaton, returning from his evening chores, saw him, spoke to him, and called him by name. Rufus knew he must do better at hiding so he went over to Tolar Thompson's farm and hid in the abandoned well, waiting for the opportune time to do his dastardly deed. This would have worked except that, at about nine-thirty, Mr. Thompson saw him, recognized him, and asked him what he was doing. Rufus said that he was hiding from some friends. Was this the truth? Of course not. The facts tell you that and the facts don't lie.

"Rufus walked back up to the house where he retrieved his father's gun that he had already secreted from the house and hidden. This was the same rifle with which he was seen practicing to hone his skills to do this cowardly act. In the dark of the night, knowing that William would at this time be reading his Bible by candlelight, Rufus walked up to the kitchen window and shot him dead. He then walked away from the window leaving telltale footprints, threw the gun into the garden and returned to hiding. The facts tell us that and the facts don't lie.

"Rufus returned to the family home at ten-thirty, the alarm having been given, to find the family, neighbours and Sheriff Chandler. What did he do? He asked, calm as you please, 'Have the Indians killed my father?' Another falsehood to cover up his actions. When some questioned his lack of sorrow he told them that he didn't care. Then the prevarications came fast and furious. He was asked about where he had been. He told five different accounts to try to cover his real whereabouts. Asked about the murder weapon, he claimed not to recognize it. But we know that he did. Asked about the slugs, he denied any knowledge of them. He later admitted they were his father's. He then said that he hadn't touched that gun, but we know that wasn't true. He had been seen practicing with it. The facts tell you that and they don't lie.

"Rufus left more at the Fawcett farm than a slug for his father. He left those tracks, those footprints. A prominent bootmaker in your community identified the footprints as having been made by a pair of boots that he made with a special, unique mark for one person and one person only, Rufus Fawcett. The facts tell us that and they don't lie.

"Now why would Rufus Fawcett commit this patricide? That is very simple. He didn't like the idea that his sister stood to inherit half of the estate. He believed that this was his property and his property alone. Furthermore, his father was not enthralled with Rufus's choice of young ladies. So what did Rufus do? He shot his father. He is a killer and your job, gentlemen of the jury, is to convict him.

"Any fool can see he is guilty and I trust that there are no fools in Sackville.

"Thank you."

Edward Morse slowly left his seat beside Rufus Fawcett. He tugged at his left ear while he took time to look at each member of the jury. These men were farmers, fishermen, lumbermen, trappers, shopkeepers. He examined their weathered faces, the lines and wrinkles etched by too many days in the cold and the rain and the sun and the wind. They were workers. Many of them couldn't read, most of them couldn't write. They were unsophisticated but not stupid. They lacked cunning but they were wise. They were guileless but not naive. They were honest, hard-working citizens who cared about people.

Edward Morse recalled the last thing that Sarah Fawcett had said to him, "Remember who your audience is." With a shrug he folded his notes, his prearranged speech, and put them in his pocket and turned to face the jury for the last time.

"Mr. Shannon tells you that facts don't lie. Gentlemen, Mr. Shannon is a much smarter man than you are and definitely a lot sharper than I am, so I guess that we are expected to take his word for everything and not question the facts. After all, facts don't lie.

"Let me give you some facts. Water does not run uphill. Yet, twice a day, not far from here, I have sat and watched the water of the Saint John River change direction and do just that, going against everything that I know about gravity. But facts don't lie so I guess it doesn't really happen. At least that is what Mr. Timothy Shannon would have you believe.

"Let me give you another fact. Water seeks its own level. It flows. Yet I have stood and watched a solid wall of water, six feet high, travel up the Petitcodiac River — a wall of water. But water can't do that. Facts don't lie so I guess the tidal bore just doesn't happen. At least that is what Mr. Timothy Shannon would have you believe.

"We all know that water freezes in winter. Somebody better tell those ships that go in and out of the harbour at Saint John Bay all winter, because they don't know that. I've seen them and so have you. But facts don't lie, so it can't be happening. At least that is what Mr. Timothy Shannon would have you believe.

"I won't tell you what to believe. I want you to think, to review everything in this case and make up your own minds. Otherwise, we wouldn't need juries, we could just have Mr. Timothy Shannon decide all the cases for us.

"We know facts aren't always correct. A good number of you think that you can hold back the sea and plant crops in the ocean bottom. Now the facts would seem to say that is not possible. You better not tell Tolar Thompson that. He thinks he can do just that and raise some pretty darn good hay.

"Forget the facts of this case for a minute. A big city lawyer can make facts tell you anything he wants. You know Rufus Fawcett. Does it seem possible for a young boy seventeen years of age to murder his father, especially when his father was as fine a man as William Fawcett? If you say, 'no,' then find him innocent. Does it seem sensible for a boy seventeen to murder his father because his father doesn't want him to marry someone whom the father has never met? If you say, 'no,' then find him innocent. From what you know of William and Sarah Fawcett, is it reasonable that they would raise a son who would murder one of them because he didn't want to share with his sister? If you say, 'no,' then find him innocent.

"I don't think you are fools, gentlemen. But the difference between Mr. Shannon and me is I am not going to treat you like fools. You have heard some church people, some teachers, some members of your community, speak up for Rufus Fawcett. That's good enough for me. If I have to believe them or the Crown, I think that I would prefer to believe them.

After all, isn't it this same Crown that wants to tax you for every acre of land that you have?

"I respect you people of Sackville and trust you to make the right decision. This is your town. This is your responsibility. Rufus Fawcett is one of your own. You decide.

"Thank you."

There was a hush as the jurors were led away followed by a hobbling Judge Jonathan Bliss. Rufus, the same calm look on his face, was escorted out by the Sheriff to wait by himself. James put a hand on Edward's shoulder. The spectators, completely silent, filed out in an orderly fashion.

Edward Morse sat at the defense table. He was exhausted. It was over, at least his part was over. There was nothing more that he could do. It was out of his hands. He put his head down on the table and slept.

For some, it was hard to believe that the jury had reviewed this case and was prepared to issue a verdict after just two hours. However, Judge Bliss had said it two days ago, "This is not a tough case."

Edward Morse was still at the same table. Everyone filled the courtroom. There was no need for benches because the entire group was standing as was Rufus Fawcett.

Despite the large number present, there was not a noise as Josiah Hicks stood to read the verdict. Josiah played it to the hilt. This was to be his finest hour and he was going to be sure that he relished every bit of it. He looked around and smiled to his family. He held a paper in front of himself, but some said that it might have been upside down because he couldn't read anyway.

James felt her hand slip into his as they stood in silence. He gave a little squeeze. How had it come to this? How had he let it come to this? All his life he had taken charge, gained control, and now he was helpless. He had let them down. A life rested in someone else's hands and he could do no more.

His wife looked up into his eyes and attempted a smile. Her weak attempt was somehow pathetic in its failure, yet, her face reflected such strength. He depended on that strength, relied on it, lived for it. At the same time, the sparkle and the tenderness still shone through. He always felt that it was her eyes. God he loved her. Why was it so hard to tell her that?

Looking at the woman on his other side, he marveled at the similarities — the raven black hair, the way the corners of their mouths threatened to turn up into a grin at the tiniest opportunity and the eyes. People said that she was her mother's daughter, and it was because of the eyes.

In only three short days, he become familiar with this room as they sat behind the wooden railing like cattle watching life on the other side of the fence. How many other sweaty hands had gripped this same bar, waiting for twelve men to decide a destiny?

It was the waiting, the same thoughts and the same questions permeating every second, every minute and every hour. The last two hours had been the worst — not knowing, just waiting.

The judge motioned to the foreman, who stood, a grave look on his face. Three days ago there had been no Josiah Hicks, this little man with the wispy gray hair who was now the centre of attention. Josiah was enjoying his moment, savouring the respect of everyone who stared at him in this crowded courtroom.

"May we have the verdict?"

"We, the members of the jury find Rufus Fawcett not guilty." There was complete silence.

Finally one of the people at the back yelled out, "Josiah. Did you say 'guilty' or 'not guilty'?"

"I said 'innocent; not guilty'."

Pandemonium broke loose. There were shouts and cries, screams and yells. Judge Bliss escaped by his private door. It is difficult to say whether the shouting was in favour of the verdict or against it, perhaps it was neither. Perhaps it was merely surprise. Sarah and the family wept.

Sarah hugged Edward Morse. She hugged her family.

What was Rufus's reaction? He turned to Morse and asked, "Buy you a drink?" That was exactly where Rufus headed. As soon as he was discharged from the custody of the court, he headed to the nearest public house where he called for a pint of brandy to treat his companions. They pounded him and congratulated him and called for more drinks. There was much glee in that tavern on that day.

That same evening Rufus and twelve special guests filed into dinner. They had a fine meal of roast beef, Yorkshire pudding, potatoes, sweet new peas and carrots. Dessert was Rufus's favourite, apple pie. No expense was spared and the wine flowed freely. Josiah Hicks spoke for the others when he toasted Rufus and thanked him for the delicious meal. Certainly, it was delicious. The Widow Evans had been expecting them.

Epilogue

The colourful leaves of autumn surrendered to the winds and cold, leaving a bleak landscape that anticipated the snow. The bay had changed from blue to a gray-green which already made it look frigid and icy.

Judges Jeremiah Botsford and Andrew Bliss remained good friends and visited each other often. On only one occasion did they ever discuss the Fawcett case.

"Andy, I know our deal was that if Rufus was found guilty, you were going to be lenient with him. You didn't go farther than that did you?"

"I am happy the boy was found not guilty. It may not have been the correct verdict but I have no doubt that it was the right one."

"What were your instructions to the jury?"

"Judge, I am surprised that you would even ask me. I thought that you knew me better than that. Pass the port, please."

Sometime after the trial, Will mentioned to his father, "Apparently Jake Oulton came into a substantial amount of money and moved away, maybe to Upper Canada, before the verdict was announced."

"I don't see that happening, Will. Jake was an opportunist but he drank all the money he ever earned as soon as he could get to a tavern."

"Do you think maybe he stole it?"

"If it were that much money, someone would have reported losing it and, to my knowledge, that's never happened."

Josiah Hicks made it a rule to never discuss the case although some of the regulars at the tavern said that he did allude to the verdict one night after having been sufficiently lubricated by the spirit of choice.

"Josiah, how'd you folks ever find that Rufus not guilty?"

"Now, Albert, you know I don't want to talk about that." He took a long swallow of the rum and looked deep into the flagon. "You know that hound of mine — the best damn hunting dog in the parish bar none, great nose, soft mouth? Well, I remember once when he was just a pup, the little bugger bit me, broke clear through the skin — hurt, too. Albert, you were there. As I recall, you wanted me to shoot that dog then and there — said he'd never be no good. Now, ain't that the same hound you wanted me to sell you last week?

Albert nodded slowly and ran his finger through the wet on the table.

"Do you remember what I did to that dog? I kicked the shit out of him and he never did it again. Now what if my only choice was shoot the dog or forget it and do nothing? Which would you advise me to do?"

Albert didn't answer, he didn't have to answer, for he knew the right choice. They called for more drinks.

A couple of weeks after the trial, Elizabeth noticed that a leather bag belonging to James was missing from the chest in their room. She knew that this bag was James's and for the sixteen years that he had worked for William Fawcett, he had saved every shilling of the pay that he had received and had put the money in the bag. He always said that it was for something really special and that he would know when that time came. Betsy never asked James about the missing bag or the money and he never volunteered to tell her.

One night in bed, he turned to her and said, "You said that you would tell me how you felt about Rufus once the trial was over."

"I still am not sure. I think that there is little doubt about his guilt or innocence. In a way I feel sorry for him because he tried so hard for father's love. For me it was given so freely."

"I'll always be curious if that bullet was meant for me. I sometimes think that things might have turned out differently if I hadn't come to live here."

"I am not sure they would have, James. Rufus would have found some other reason to destroy himself. Do you ever wonder why he was declared innocent? Was Edward Morse that good?"

"Or was Timothy Shannon that bad? I think he concentrated on facts rather than people. When you think of his case, he spent a lot of time on opportunity and less on motive. The people around here certainly didn't like him. He was too slick, too polished, too condescending."

Elizabeth sat up. "I wonder if the community just couldn't believe that a boy of seventeen could murder his father."

"Couldn't believe it or wouldn't believe it? They knew what would happen to him if he were found guilty. Maybe it was preferable to set a murderer free, than to send a young man to the gallows."

"One thing is certain. I am glad that you came to our farm. I don't know how father would have managed without you; I don't know how I would have managed without you."

Johnnie came over to check on Sarah one evening and they sat at the large pine table where so much of the life of the farm had centred.

"What will you do now, Sarah?"

"The farm is Elizabeth and James's now. I will live here with them. Hopefully they will keep me busy with grandchildren as your children have done for you."

"I miss him, Sarah." Johnnie looked around the room for signs of his brother.

"He loved you, Johnnie. You must accept that this is no longer Fawcett farm. It will be handed down through the George family — the children of James and Elizabeth."

John nodded his understanding. With his hands behind his head, he leaned back in the chair. "Sarah, I could never account for Rufus's behaviour during the trial. He was so calm and unbothered."

"I have no answers and have thought about it myself. Maybe he needed William's love and approval so much that when he realized it was never to be, he gave up. He did not care any more."

"I suspect that his demeanor was one of the influences which affected the jury. Perhaps they didn't believe a guilty person could or would behave like that."

"He has always been a complex child, difficult to know and difficult to understand. I believe that part of him will never change."

After to the acquittal, additional information came to light. There was further proof that Rufus had indeed killed his father and there was a move to retry him for murder. When this information reached the farm, Sarah took Rufus to John Thompson's place where he hid for the winter.

In the spring, Rufus moved to the States and never returned to his home in Sackville. Someone later reported that they had visited him in Florida, but that was never confirmed. It was rumoured that he had made a lot of money and had moved to New England, but neither was there any proof of that. Family historians have unearthed no information about Rufus or about possible descendants.

New Brunswick Royal Gazette
September 26, 1832

On the sixth instant, at the Circuit Court held at Westmorland, Rufus Fawcett, a young man about 18 years of age, was arraigned and tried before the Hon. Judge Bliss, for the alleged murder of Mr. William Fawcett, his father. The circumstances which caused suspicion to fall upon his son, chiefly transpired at the Coroner's Inquest, and were shortly after related to us by a person who was present on the occasion; but as the trial was then pending we abstained from laying them before the public. The trial now being over, we give them in substance as follows: — Mr. William Fawcett, the deceased, was a substantial farmer near Sackville, a man of unblemished character and universally esteemed. He had but two children, one a daughter, who was married, the other a son, Rufus, who was residing at home with his father. On some occasion, the deceased had intimated an intention, at his death, to divide his property equally between his son and daughter — this was understood to have given offence to the son. Rufus was paying attention to a young woman in the neighbourhood, which did not meet the full approbation of his father, and in reference to this circumstance, the father had said, that he had not pledged himself as to the manner in which he would finally dispose of his property. The latter circumstances were known to have produced farther dissatisfaction in the mind of his son. Rufus had said to some of the neighbours, that in a few months there would be a great overturn in the house of his father. This was understood by the neighbours to imply that Rufus had intended to marry, and take his wife home to his father's, and that the young people would take the management of affairs. In this manner matters stood, previous to the evening of the melancholy catastrophe.

About 10 o'clock, on the evening of the day when it happened, after having had family prayer, the son being absent, the father continued sitting at the table, reading in a book of sermons, when the shot which terminated his existence was fired in at the window. He instantly expired without saying one word, but continued upright in the chair, except that his head drooped. An alarm was immediately given, and after a number of the neighbours had collected together, who were all deeply affected, Rufus entered. Without apparent emotion, he asked what was the matter, and upon being told that his father was shot, he asked, — 'have the Indians killed my father?' — The apparent absence of every degree of that concern and anxiety which might naturally be expected in an affectionate son, towards his deceased and respected father, especially under such circumstances, together with an indescribable something in his whole manner, not otherwise to be accountable for, made an impression on the minds of one or more of the persons present — This impression was communicated to others and finally to himself, and to which he replied with an air of strong indifference, 'I do not care what any person thinks.' He was then interrogated as to where he was when the deed was done, but he could not give any satisfactory account of himself. He had left home on horseback, before dusk, for the purpose he said of going to the Marsh, distant some miles, to see if any cattle or pigs were in it, and to drive them away. He was also seen returning, sooner than it was possible for him to have done had he gone to the marsh — Upon searching, the gun with which the deed was done was found thrown over the fence into the garden, and was identified by the neighbours as belonging to the Fawcett family. At first he denied all knowledge of the gun. Afterwards he admitted that it belonged to the house, but he had not had it in his hands for a long time previous; whereas some of the persons present had seen it in his hands about a fortnight before. In the wound or about the person of the deceased was found one or more slugs. Rufus was asked if he had any such slugs in his possession, and he said that he had not. He was then asked for the key of his chest, and when that was opened, a number of slugs similar to that in the wound was found in his chest.

The ground was examined from the road to the window in at which the shot was fired, and the track of a person was distinctly visible, approaching to the window backwards, and receding and then approaching a second time. Rufus' boot was then applied to the track, and was found to correspond exactly with it. In the track was visible a peculiar stamp and the same peculiar stamp was present upon the sole of his boot. The shoemaker who made the boot was present, and he certified, that he had put that peculiar stamp on Rufus' boots, but he had never put the stamp on any other boot or shoe, which had gone out of his shop.

During the investigation by the Coroner's Jury, every person except Rufus was deeply affected at the melancholy fate of the deceased. Rufus alone did not manifest any emotion or concern upon the occasion; and it was only when finally he was taken into custody to be removed to the Gaol that he was seen to shed a few tears.

At the trial a great concourse of people were assembled from all parts of the surrounding country. To the Judge and to all present it was a solemn and affecting scene — indeed the very thought of a young man 18 years of age, being even suspected of the murder of his father (a man so universally esteemed that it was thought he had not one enemy in the world) but much more to see him standing at the bar of his country to take his trial upon such a charge must have been completely overwhelming — But Rufus, the person implicated, and who in every point of view was most deeply of all concerned, continued to manifest the same insensibility and indifference. At the awful moment — that moment when the Jury returned to the Court, and when the hearts of so numerous an assemblage of people were palpating in breathless anxiety to hear the verdict which in all possibility would seal his doom — even at that moment when the unhappy young man was suspended — hair hung over the pit of death, he remained as unconcerned as ever.

We are not aware of the nature of the evidence adduced on the trial, but we understand that even when the Jurors pronounced their Verdict 'NOT GUILTY," it created very general surprise.

We are farther informed, that the first act of this young man after being discharged from the custody of the Court, was to go into a public house nearby, and call for a pint of brandy to treat his companions, and that same evening he treated the Jurors to a supper.

Afterword

I became aware of the Fawcett murder in a book called *The Chignecto Connexion*, by P. Penner, which my older brother, Fred, purchased at the United Church in Sackville. It was a story that had never been talked about in our family.

As I searched for my family roots, I joined some of the genealogy lists run by Rootsweb on the Internet. The people on the New Brunswick and Nova Scotia lists were most friendly and eager to help. It was through this source that I began to correspond, by email, with Kathy Lewis of Fredericton, NB, who was in the process of compiling a history of the Fawcett family: William Fawcett, the victim in this book, was one of three brothers who came to the Chignecto region of Atlantic Canada from Yorkshire in 1774. Kathy willingly shared her research and answered all my silly questions.

Through Sandra Devlin, who writes a self-syndicated column appearing in nine Maritimes newspapers, a query was placed in "Missing Links." Almost immediately, correspondence began with Nancy (George) Gray and Moira (George) Lawrence, also third great grandchildren of William Fawcett. They filled in many of the blanks and added their family's spin on the story.

The main sources of information were the inscription on the gravestone (affectionately known as "The Murder Stone") and the two *New Brunswick Royal Gazette* newspaper articles. One of these articles was written at the time of the murder and the other was written after Rufus's trial. These formed the framework around which the story was written.

However, this is a novel and it is historical fiction. No one really knows who said what or who did what. Several books and references became the foundation for these events. *History of Sackville, New Brunswick* by W.C. Milner was most useful in providing the flavour and events of the times and the town. In an attempt to add realism, I based many of the characters' names on persons alive at the time and ascribed traits that I hope will not cause offense to the readers.

For a taste of what it was like to be a settler in early Canada and a selection of actual anecdotes recorded by these pioneers, I would recommend *When The Work's All Done This Fall* by Dave McIntosh. Fascinating reading, it provides a taste of life on the farms across Canada as well as the background for some of the events in my book.

My grandfather, William Gideon Closson, recorded a series of short stories that he called *Grandfather Tales*. I was too young to appreciate these while he was alive but some of them, such as the training of the ox, the sheep shearing, the stoneboat, the horseride to get the cattle, and butchering day, were his experiences. I can vividly remember him telling me that a sharp knife is safer than a dull one.

Some of the incidents come from my own experiences. I used personal observations from years in an English-style boarding school for the events that happened to James George. I have participated in horseshoeing and beekeeping. My grandfather taught me to make a whistle. Every year I go deer hunting with my family and we are still tracking the "Gray Ghost."

When I began this project, I had no idea where it would go or how it would end. As the story unfolded, I did develop an understanding and sympathy for Rufus. Undoubtedly, he committed the murder but can hardly be described as a "monster in human shape."

Conversations about the book inevitably lead others to reveal a "black sheep story" in their past. Every genealogist has one. It is a fascinating tableau within which to study relationships, history and geography.

> — Robert James
> Wasaga Beach, Ontario
> February 2000

A Selection of Our Titles in Print

Title	ISBN	Price
A Lad from Brantford (David Adams Richards) essays	0-921411-25-1	11.95
All the Other Phil Thompsons Are Dead (Phil Thompson) poetry	1-896647-05-7	12.95
A View from the Bucket: A Grand Lake and McNabs Island Memoir (Jean Redekopp) memoir, history	0-921411-52-9	14.95
Best in Life: A Guide to Managing Your Relationships ... (Ted Mouradian) self-help, business	0-921411-55-3	18.69
CHSR Poetry Slam (Andrew Titus, ed) poetry	1-896647-06-5	10.95
Combustible Light (Matt Santateresa) poetry	0-921411-97-9	12.95
Cover Makes a Set (Joe Blades) poetry	0-919957-60-9	8.95
Crossroads Cant (Mary Elizabeth Grace, Mark Seabrook, Shafiq, Ann Shin. Joe Blades, editor) poetry	0-921411-48-0	13.95
Dark Seasons (Georg Trakl; Robin Skelton, trans.) poetry	0-921411-22-7	10.95
Dividing the Fire (Robert B. Richards) poetry	1-896647-15-4	4.95
Elemental Mind (K.V. Skene) poetry	1-896647-16-2	10.95
for a cappuccino on Bloor (kath macLean) poetry	0-921411-74-X	13.95
Gift of Screws (Robin Hannah) poetry	0-921411-56-1	12.95
Heart-Beat of Healing (Denise DeMoura) poetry	1-896647-27-8	4.95
Heaven of Small Moments (Allan Cooper) poetry	0-921411-79-0	12.95
Herbarium of Souls (Vladimir Tasic) short fiction	0-921411-72-3	14.95
I Hope It Don't Rain Tonight (Phillip Igloliorti) poetry	0-921411-57-X	11.95
Like Minds (Shannon Friesen) short fiction	0-921411-81-2	14.95
Manitoba highway map (rob mclennan) poetry	0-921411-89-8	13.95
Memories of Sandy Point, St. George's Bay, Newfoundland (Phyllis Pieroway) memoir, history	0-921411-33-2	14.95
New Power (Christine Lowther) poetry	0-921411-94-4	11.95
Notes on drowning (rob mclennan) poetry	0-921411-75-8	13.95
Open 24 Hours (Anne Burke, D.C. Reid, Brenda Niskala Joe Blades, rob mclennan) poetry	0-921411-64-2	13.95
Railway Station (karl wendt) poetry	0-921411-82-0	11.95
Reader Be Thou Also Ready (Robert James) novel	1-896647-26-X	18.69
Rum River (Raymond Fraser) short fiction	0-921411-61-8	16.95
Seeing the World with One Eye (Edward Gates) poetry	0-921411-69-3	12.95
ShadowyTechnicians: New Ottawa Poets (rob mclennan, ed.)	0-921411-71-5	16.95
Song of the Vulgar Starling (Eric Miller) poetry	0-921411-93-6	14.95
Speaking Through Jagged Rock (Connie Fife) poetry	0-921411-99-5	12.95
Tales for an Urban Sky (Alice Major) poetry	1-896647-11-1	13.95
The Curse of Gutenberg (Dan Daniels)	1-896647-23-5	16.95
The Longest Winter (Julie Doiron, Ian Roy) photos & fiction	0-921411-95-2	18.69
Túnel de proa verde / Tunnel of the Green Prow (Nela Rio; Hugh Hazelton, translator) poetry	0-921411-80-4	13.95
Wharves and Breakwaters of Yarmouth County, Nova Scotia (Sarah Petite) art, travel	1-896647-13-8	17.95
What Morning Illuminates (Suzanne Hancock) poetry	1-896647-18-9	4.95
What Was Always Hers (Uma Parameswaran) short fiction	1-896647-12-X	17.95

www.brokenjaw.com hosts our current catalogue, submissions guidelines, maunscript award competitions, booktrade sales representation and distribution information. Directly from us, all individual orders must be prepaid. All Canadian orders must add 7% GST/HST (Canada Customs and Revenue Agency Number: 12489 7943 RT0001). **BROKEN JAW PRESS, Box 596 Stn A, Fredericton NB E3B 5A6, Canada.**